TUMBLE

V. V. SIDOLI

Matador
Unit E2 Airfield Business Park,
Harrison Road, Market Harborough,
Leicestershire. LE16 7UL
Tel: 0116 2792299
Email: books@troubador.co.uk
Web: www.troubador.co.uk/matador
Twitter: @matadorbooks

ISBN 978 1805140 665

British Library Cataloguing in Publication Data.
A catalogue record for this book is available from the British Library.

Printed and bound in Great Britain by 4edge Limited
Typeset in 11pt Adobe Caslson Pro by Troubador Publishing Ltd, Leicester, UK

Matador is an imprint of Troubador Publishing Ltd

For Celeste Sidoli
1895 – 1955

AUTHOR'S NOTE

The story contained in this book is based on historical events. As a novel it inevitably includes some re-imagining of a number of details. The central characters are fictitious, but there are some named individuals, such as Major Braybrook (who actually was in charge at Warth Mills), whose involvement is based on real events, but whose detailed actions and words have also been imagined.

Cesare Bianchi's story is based on information provided by his family to The Warth Mills Project. His direct involvement with the central characters and his words have both been imagined and I am very grateful to his son, Robert, for providing both his consent and his trust.

Otherwise, all characters and events in this book, other than those in the public domain, are fictitious and any resemblance to real persons, living or dead, is purely coincidental.

My grandfather also made the journey from Bardi to South Wales and was interned during the Second World War. Mercifully, he was not one of those who found themselves on the SS Arandora Star. I have tried to describe the events leading to the tragic loss of so many of those who did set sail on 1 July 1940 as accurately as possible, drawing from reports and materials now widely available to those who search.

In truth, I struggled to decide whether I could write about those terrible events in the form of a novel, whilst maintaining the solemn respect the victims deserve. In the end, I concluded that this was a story worth trying to tell. I can only hope you might agree.

ONE

Italy – 1921

Emiliano was a voracious reader; always hungry for more. By the age of thirteen he had read much of what he could find nearby and he was beginning to widen his search. This morning, as he had daily for the last month, he was heading to Grezzo, a small village just a short distance northwest of his home town of Bardi.

It was the start of May and the early mornings were still light and fresh before the advance of summer's density. As he headed out along the road towards the edge of town, he could feel the sun rising against his back as it spilled over the top of the ancient castle that dominated Bardi's skyline. Luca, as ever, led the way; his nose, as ever, led Luca.

As this walk had been repeated over the course of the preceding weeks, what started as a three kilometre march along the road, became a more varied journey into the surrounding woods and hills. The departures from the road began as a deliberate deviation to prevent Emiliano's eagerness bringing him to Leonardo's door prematurely each day, but now they had become an added early morning joy for the companions as they explored different routes through the trees.

This morning their route took them along the road until the rooftops of the houses in Grezzo could be seen and then they headed right and into the trees. In the near distance, the imposing steep slopes of the Apennines stood pale in the morning light, but the lower rolling tree covered slopes that preceded their scree provided the ideal route into the valley that led to the rear of Leonardo's home.

Each morning, Luca had become as eager as Emiliano to set forth on their journey. Whilst the destination was the source of excitement for Emiliano, for Luca it was always the trek through the trees. As they set out daily, Luca succumbed to his instinctive obsessions as he checked the key points along the streets leading out of town, bestowing each with a sniff and a shower. At first he had been prone to emptying his bladder long before they reached the last building in town, although that did not stop him lifting his leg with only vaporous results. Before the end of the first week, however, Emiliano noticed with admiration that Luca had achieved equal apportionment of his offering between the keystones of his kingdom.

Once beyond the town's built limits, Luca's undivided attention was upwards towards Emiliano, looking for the slightest indication that they had reached the morning's point of departure from the road. On making the turn, his attention returned like a magnet to the earth, his nose determining the zig zag of their progress through the trees whilst the metronomic swing of his tail set the pace.

Luca had chosen his willing companion some three years earlier. He had tip toed into the yard early one morning looking for food and after a rigorous vetting programme in which he tested Emiliano's skills in play, food provision and, most importantly, his willingness to find new places to explore, he decided to give him the job. After that, they were inseparable.

Emiliano tried, only half heartedly, to find out where Luca had come from. In truth, it was not unusual to see occasional strays wander from the countryside into town. Sometimes, they had been abandoned by owners who could no longer afford to feed them. In the hills they were used as hunting dogs, but the poverty and increasing age of their owners could lead to ill health or infirmity and with those came an end to hunting and sufficient food for the dogs. Emiliano had heard stories of loyal dogs being found next to their owners long after they had died and he sometimes wondered, given his devotion to Emiliano, why Luca would have moved on. But he was also aware that the hill dogs could sometimes face cruelty at the hands of desperate masters who saw the animal as no more than a necessary tool in the hunt for a meal.

When Luca arrived in the yard three years ago his black coat was tangled and knotted. He bore no immediate signs of injury, but despite his thick coat it was clear that he was painfully thin. The wary step back he took as Emiliano emerged into the yard, was accompanied by an enquiring look in his eyes which suggested his first instinct was to give this human a chance before reaching judgment. In time Emiliano concluded that Luca had encountered human kindness before and whatever the circumstances of his journey to town, his intelligence had driven his decisions along the way.

Emiliano was at first unsure of his grandmother's reaction to Luca's decision to stay, but Luca quickly identified the route to Nonna's heart and somehow she managed to find a little extra food each day from the little they had.

Luca's breed was indistinct. He appeared to be a mix of many of those to be found in the hills and his skills were as varied as his genes. His powerful hind legs helped him leap into trees in pursuit of squirrels – more like a cat than a dog – and his speed across the ground meant that he could suddenly disappear in a blur into the trees only to appear again almost silently at Emiliano's side when his playful pursuits were done. It was at his nose, however, that the best of his genes had clustered. As he rose each morning and entered the yard, he would stand stock still and raise his nose to the air, taking his time to take in all that was happening around him. He drew in not only the smells of the present, but also the scent of what had already taken place that morning – the early departure of Signor di Marco with his dogs heading for his goats in the hills, the baking of bread at *il Forno* and old Salvatore Conti's cigarette smoke as he welcomed sunrise through a nicotine haze from his balcony three streets away. Luca's stillness would linger as he took his time to draw in the morning air and only when he was satisfied that all was as it should be, would he lean forward and stretch the powerful hind muscles that had been recoiled during sleep.

As they headed through the trees that morning, Luca was quickly onto the scent of a squirrel. In an instant, he was gone. Emiliano maintained his direction in the knowledge that Luca would soon return to his side, but today his absence grew longer. Emiliano called him, but he did not appear; something, Emiliano concluded, had captured Luca's attention. He stopped in his tracks and to his left heard what sounded like the steady fall of stones and earth upon the woodland floor. In between the stone patter, he then heard occasional determined mutterings which unmistakeably came from Luca. Emiliano followed the sounds and quickly came upon Luca at the foot of a tree digging frantically with his front paws barely ahead of his burrowing nose. As he approached Luca and commanded him to step aside, he saw nothing at first in the narrow excavation, but then at the shallow base he saw the unmistakeable texture and colour of a truffle, just like the illustrations he had seen in Nonna's cookery book.

Emiliano Magnani was born to Francesco and Adelina in 1908. His parents had known each other since childhood having both been born to local families. There was never any doubt they would marry one day as they proved inseparable through their teenage years. When Adelina fell pregnant soon after their marriage, there was only joy in their lives. They both wanted a large family and they spoke of Emi being the first of four, or maybe six, siblings. Francesco had plans.

The repressive Pelloux government had fallen in 1900. In the same year, following the assassination of King Umberto I, Victor Emmanuel III came to the throne and supported the return of constitutional government. In 1903 Giovanni Giolitti began the second of five terms as Prime Minister, during which he introduced social reforms. There was optimism in the air of north Italy, although less so in the south where protest and repression persisted.

They had both lived through poverty for much of their young lives, but Francesco was determined to make a better life for his young wife and their children. He foresaw opportunities in agriculture. There was talk of state subsidised irrigation and land reclamation schemes in the Po valley and he hoped those would eventually lead to similar benefits for land along the River Ceno nearby.

On 19 February 1908, Francesco held his new born son in his arms. His tears were uncontained. The overwhelming joy he had anticipated was instead suffocated by the agonising grief he felt at Adelina's death in childbirth; it was as if the ground beneath him had disappeared and he was falling. As he fell he told Emi through his tears of the love his parents would always have for him.

Francesco did his best for his son, but his spirit was broken and his optimism appeared to be irrecoverably extinguished. He and Emi lived with Francesco's mother, Maria, and her kindness and steely resolve formed the bedrock of their day to day existence. Francesco had four older siblings, but whilst he and Adelina had always been devoted to a life in their home town, economic hardship had led to the emigration of each sibling over time. Two brothers and a sister with her husband had made new lives in America, whilst Agostino had followed his uncle to South Wales. They were each able to send back some money from time to time and it was Nonna's careful management of those funds that enabled her to support her grieving son and Emi during those difficult years.

Giolitti resigned in March 1914. When war broke out, the new conservative government, led by Antonio Salandra, took an apparent position of neutrality, but behind the scenes negotiations were taking place with both sides. Territory was on offer – Austria proposed Trentino become Italy's, but France, Britain and Russia made a better offer and in April 1915 they secretly signed the Treaty of London leading in May to Italy joining the war against Austria-Hungary.

Francesco was conscripted. He was a man of peace not war and few could understand the cause they were being asked to fight for. He was present at the disastrous battle of Caporetto and suffered lung damage in a German gas attack. He returned to Bardi with his body as broken as his failing spirit.

More than six hundred thousand Italians died in the war. In the two years that followed, it was estimated that the same number died in four waves of the influenza pandemic. Francesco's weakened lungs could not withstand the virus; he died in the winter of 1919.

Emi was eleven when his father died; only the embrace of his grandmother ensured that the explosion he felt inside was contained. The loss of his mother had been explained to Emi by Nonna in gentle stages as he grew, couched always in terms of how much he was wanted and loved by his parents.

His father had done his best to answer Emi's questions, but his responses were usually limited to his showing Emi the photograph of Adelina he always kept in his pocket and telling him how proud she would be of him if she were here now. Emi could see the pain in his father's eyes and such was his continuing fragility that Emi chose no longer to speak of his mother with him for fear of breaking what was left of his father's heart. In later life he regretted that decision, believing that he might have used those difficult talks to find a way together through his father's grief. But he was young and he could not bear to see his father's pain.

The instinctive attraction that his parents had to a life rich in family numbers, was felt by Emi too, as was the empty feeling left by its absence. Adelina had lost both her parents at a young age and her only brother had been a fisherman when lost at sea. The departure of Emi's paternal aunt and uncles to foreign lands left him wondering about the nephews and nieces he had never met.

It was thus his widowed grandmother who became from Emi's birth the source of all the nutrients of family life and support that he needed. Her devotion to Emi was absolute. It was she who recognised Emi's love of the written word and encouraged him in his reading. She wondered whether in books he found an opportunity to escape the sadness of his own story.

Maria had grown up in a time when illiteracy was the norm for the majority of the Italian population. It was not until 1877 that two years of primary education was made compulsory. She learnt to read through the kindness of the daughter of a wealthy landowner in Piacenza. Maria worked in the house as a cook and when Isabella saw her one day absorbed in the illustrations of one of the cookery books in the kitchen, it quickly became clear that the text of the recipes was a mystery that Maria was longing to solve. With patience Isabella taught Maria to master the words and Maria repaid her kindness when her new found skill unlocked her ability to translate the recipes into delicious dishes for the family and their well healed guests. When Maria left to move back to Bardi after her marriage three years later, Isabella gave her the cookery book. It was that book which became Emi's favourite as Nonna taught him to read.

T W O

Emi had first met Leonardo Carpanini in April 1921. He had made his way to the main square in Bardi and was exploring the morning's market stalls when he spotted a man sat at a table drinking coffee whilst reading a book. The man's jacket was worn at the collar and elbows and as he sipped his coffee or occasionally ran his hand through his dark beard, his gaze through metal rimmed glasses remained fixed on the contents of his book. His absorption in what he read quickly pricked Emi's curiosity.

He circled around the back of the market stalls and was able to position himself behind the man's shoulder as he strained to try and see what he was reading. The text was not large and Emi found himself daring to move ever closer in his attempt to identify the words.

'Would you like to borrow my glasses?' asked the reader without shifting his gaze from the book. Emi took half a step back, annoyed with himself for being so bold. He did not know what to say.

'Come and sit down,' the man said 'and tell me why you

are so interested in the Parthian Empire.' When there was no reaction he continued 'You *are* interested in the Parthian Empire aren't you?'

Hesitantly, Emi responded 'I might be,' whilst not having the faintest idea what it was.

The man turned to look at Emi for the first time, removing his glasses and taking in the boy who stood before him. He could see he was embarrassed by his predicament. The man stood and held out his hand. As Emi nervously shook it, the man introduced himself and in a gentle voice said again 'Please, have a seat.'

As Emi sat down opposite him, Leonardo noticed for the first time the black dog who immediately sat next to Emi's chair, his eyes fixed on the new character in town. 'I'm sorry,' Emi said immediately 'I did not mean to be so rude. It's just that you seemed so interested in what you were reading, I thought it must be something good.'

Leonardo smiled. 'It is good. Do you like to read?'

'Yes,' Emi replied. 'Very much.'

Only then did Emi see the crescent shaped scar below Leonardo's left eye. He tried not to focus on it, but too late for Leonardo not to notice. 'An injury from childhood,' Leonardo explained. 'Fell flat on my face reading a book and not looking where I was going!'

They spoke about some of the things they each liked to read and time slipped by before Leonardo looked at his watch and suddenly realised that he would be late for his meeting at the bank. He got up to leave, but hesitated as he picked up his book and glasses. 'I have many books. Perhaps you would like to see them one day?'

He did not expect Emi's immediate response. 'Can I see them tomorrow?'

'Well, yes. But won't you be at school?'

'It's closed again. No-one knows when it will re-open. That's the third time this year. They do their best, but there are only a few of us who turn up most of the time. All I know is that there are some arguments about how to pay for the building repairs and things like that. It's all a bit of a mess.'

Leonardo had a knowing smile on his face and said 'Alright then, but you must ask your parents first'. Emi reserved judgment on whether he might later tell Leonardo why that was not possible. They arranged to meet at Leonardo's house in Grezzo the next morning.

When Emi knocked on the door to Leonardo's home the following day, he found that he was not at all nervous, but instead was pre-occupied with his curiosity. Leonardo welcomed him into his home and smiled when he realised Emi's uninvited companion was following closely behind.

The house was not large and smelt musty. Items were scattered around as if they were recent arrivals, yet to find their place. He was led into the kitchen and invited to sit at a table which was squeezed into a corner surrounded by wooden crates laden with items yet to be un-packed. Leonardo apologised and explained that he had only just moved in. He had moved back to Grezzo from Parma within the last few days following the death of his mother whose home this had been until her health had deteriorated.

They chatted for a while, but Emi was unable to hide his eagerness to see the books. 'How many books do you have?'

Leonardo smiled. 'I hope we still have one thousand eight hundred and sixty one. Maybe you will count them for me to check?' He could see that Emi was lost for words. 'Follow me.'

Leonardo led Emi through the back of the house and into a small yard which they crossed before entering a long stone building. Inside there were a number of crates all containing books. Emi wandered among them touching the covers and trying to read the titles that were visible. Eventually, he turned to Leonardo and asked 'Are you rich? How could you afford so many books?'

Leonardo laughed. 'I am merely their custodian for a while.'

He tasked Emi in the days that followed with helping him to build shelves with planks of wood that he had found in the yard, left over from his mother's removal of a wooden drying house to create space for chickens. When the shelves were finished they placed the books carefully in their new home. In time the plan was to arrange them by subject, but for now they were placed alphabetically by author. Emi counted in all one thousand eight hundred and sixty one.

Emi looked forward to his daily visits and delighted in his task. When it came time to create a catalogue by subject, he made it a deliberately slow process and found himself uncontrollably immersed in the scent and textures of the books as much as their content. He asked Leonardo for guidance on subject matter when needed and their discussions about the books opened all kinds of opportunities to talk about their own lives. Leonardo did not seek to hurry his new friend; he could see the joy the books evoked.

Leonardo explained that twelve years ago he had moved to Parma where he had been offered his first teaching post at a school which, at one time, had been filled with senior pupils and had been much larger than he found it on arrival. It was at a time when there were endless arguments about the administration and funding of schools under municipal control. By the time of his appointment, the school had inherited a mix of primary aged and older children, but in 1911 the responsibility for running primary schools was transferred to central government and when the consequent re-organisation took place, the primary children moved to a new local school. Some of the older children also moved elsewhere, but a few remained and Leonardo continued to teach them alone until such time as places were found for them in other locations. What was supposed to be a temporary arrangement continued for three years, at which point the crumbling building could no longer safely remain open. Many of the books in the school library had been moved elsewhere over the years, but on closure some of the older books remained. There appeared to be no plan for them and when Leonardo enquired about this the authorities asked him to store the books for the time being, which he did in the cellar of the house that he was renting. He too was moved to another school when the building closed; but within weeks war descended.

Leonardo was conscripted, but could not find it within his conscience to fight. He could see no good reason for Italy to be involved in the conflict and despised the prospect of wasted lives. He resisted the call-up and kept a low profile until, late in the war, he was found and faced the prospect of a military tribunal. The process was slow in the face of more than a million men lined up for disciplinary action for various forms of resistance or desertion and he was saved by the amnesty which came after the war. When he returned to teaching he asked the authorities on a number of occasions when they would collect the books in his cellar, but he was met first with the response that someone would get back to him and then, eventually, indifference. When he knew he would be moving back to Grezzo, he tried again, but was told that there was no plan to move the books elsewhere and, frankly, they were too busy to care.

Leonardo was hesitant when he told Emi about his resistance to the war; he did not want to put their new friendship at risk and was troubled that a thirteen year old boy might simply think him a coward. He knew he was no such thing; he would fight tooth and nail for a cause he believed in.

Emi told him about his father. 'Nonna says my father was a brave man, who could never hurt another person. I think there must have been many men like that in the war, so why did they fight each other anyway?'

'I don't know Emi. Maybe it's because even the brave feel fear.'

'Nonna says it's because men don't tell each other what they truly think and if they did there would never be another war.'

Leonardo did not respond. He suspected that men speaking their minds would probably lead to more, rather than fewer wars.

—⁂—

The truffle was carefully wrapped in Emi's handkerchief when he arrived at Leonardo's home. As the door opened, Luca slipped in first and went straight to the kitchen where he knew his morning treat of a little pasta with cheese would be waiting in a bowl. Emi was quick to show Leonardo his find and he led Emi to the bookshelves where he announced that he had a book on fungi somewhere, but could not recall the author's name and thus the current order in which the books were placed could not lead them to it.

It was mid-morning before Emi found it – *'Funghi Nativi Italiani'*. The small book was filled with illustrations and descriptions of the varieties of fungi native to Italy. After much debate, Emi and Leonardo agreed that they were in possession of a white truffle of the *'Bianchetto'* or *'Tartufo Marzuolo'* variety. The text suggested that the variety had a scent of garlic and although *'not the most prestigious of truffles'*, the flavour is *'good in measured amounts'*. The variety was typically said to be found between mid January to mid April and thus Emi's find was a little late.

As Emi headed home, his first thought was to try and sell his truffle. He wanted to find a way to help Nonna with a little money. He decided he would discuss this with her as she was likely to know not only who in town might want a truffle, but also who might be able to afford it.

Nonna thanked him for his thoughtfulness, but suggested his truffle could bring more joy in its eating than in its monetary value. 'This gift of the earth should be savoured by the poor, not just the rich.' Emi took little persuading once Nonna's mind was made up; he knew she would produce something so delicious that its memory would delight his tastebuds for the rest of the year. He told Nonna that he would like to invite Leonardo to share in the meal and they agreed on the following evening for the event.

Leonardo arrived bearing wine and handpicked flowers for Nonna. She liked him immediately. To this day, Emi did not know how she did it, but from somewhere Nonna secured a small loin of pork and placed before them the simplest of dishes flavoured with delicate shavings of the truffle. Leonardo closed his eyes with the first taste and let out a small involuntary sigh. Nonna smiled silently. They all felt the warm embrace of this rare treat; all, save Luca. They had him to thank for the delicious discovery, but after inspecting the small piece of pork that Emi held in his hand under the table, he walked away, seemingly dismayed by the corruption of a tasty piece of meat. When he recalled the enthusiasm with which Luca clawed at the earth to find his prize, Emi wondered how he could be so repelled by the reward he was offered.

THREE

Emi spent as much time as he could absorbed in the *biblioteca*, as they both jokingly called it, at Leonardo's home. By the summer of 1922, the re-organisation of the books by subject matter and the accompanying catalogue were complete. Nevertheless, they continued to talk at length in the months that followed about possible adjustments and debated whether particular texts would be better placed under alternative subjects.

The most debated among these was a book about events before, during and after the battle of Adwa in 1896 at which the Italian army was defeated by the Ethiopians. Emi had read it, felt that the focus was on the battle and took the view it should remain in the military section, where he had placed it. Leonardo, on the other hand, suggested it should be in the politics section. To him, the battle marked the end of a foolish colonial policy that had led to the demise of Francesco Crispi's government.

Politics proved to be a favourite topic of conversation for the two friends. Emi had never before met anyone who appeared to know so much about what was happening in the world. But it was events closer to home that caused Leonardo both concern and increasing anger. The source of those emotions could almost always be found in the activities of '*il crotalo*', as Leonardo privately called him. He likened him to a rattlesnake because, Leonardo explained, 'Benito Mussolini has slithered from side to side through politics in pursuit of power, armed with a baby's rattle, making a lot of noise.'

'Did you know Emi that *il crotalo* used to be a socialist journalist? Hard to believe isn't it?'

But now things were becoming serious.

In March 1919, Mussolini had formed his *fasci di combattimento* in Milan and in April that year Fascists set the offices of the socialist paper *L'Avanti* alight, killing four people. Local Fascist groups were formed in the country and they set about suppressing labour unions and peasant cooperatives. Black shirted thugs used violence in pursuit of their aims. In October 1920 Fascists had entered the council chamber of the newly elected socialist administration in Bologna killing nine people.

On the back of support from many landowners and some of the cities' middle classes, in November 1921 Mussolini sought further to empower his movement through the formation of a political party – the *Partito Nazionale Fascista*. Local Fascist squad leaders now controlled parts of rural Italy and syndicates were formed to control labour.

Very few areas were able to stand against the violence of the black shirts, but Parma proved to be one. In August 1922, the *Arditi del Popolo* – 'The People's Daring Ones' – defended

Parma against a force of thousands of Fascists. Around this time, Leonardo had left Grezzo for several weeks, telling Emi he had to visit a sick relative, but when news broke of events in Parma, Emi wondered whether his friend had stood shoulder to shoulder with those who had defended the city. Leonardo did not speak of it and the victory proved hollow when in October Mussolini organised a march on Rome. Victor Emmanuel III refused his Prime Minister's request to declare martial law in a bid to avoid civil war and instead, on 29 October 1922, he asked Mussolini to form a government.

Leonardo was in despair. At first, Mussolini headed a coalition government, but Leonardo was in no doubt that *il crotalo* was weaving a path behind the scenes in pursuit of absolute power, filled with a deadly venom capable of poisoning the whole country.

In the late spring of 1923, Nonna became unwell. She suffered chest pains, which Emi suspected had begun sooner than she acknowledged and by the time she succumbed to the truth, she found herself unable to rise from her bed for several days at a time.

The doctor visited and prescribed medication. He wanted Maria to see a specialist in Bologna, but there would be a cost and although her children continued to send what little they could each month, she was adamant that she did not wish them to know that she was unwell. She sought to reassure Emi that the medication would do the trick, but he decided it was time to repay Nonna's kindness to him and he determined to seek work to pay for her treatment.

Emi's first thought was to try to find work in town, but he quickly realised that at the age of fifteen he was more likely to find farm work. He decided to approach Aldo Pavani. Nonna knew the Pavani family well; they ran a farm nearby. Emi chose his moment to speak to him when he routinely came into town on a Wednesday morning. He was sat at the same café at which Emi had first met Leonardo; this time he approached from the front.

'*Buongiorno* Signor Pavani. I hope you are well.'

'*Buongiorno* Emi. I am as well as a poor farmer can ever be. How is Maria? I understand she has not been well herself?'

'She has good and bad days, but I am worried about her and that is why I would like to speak to you. I am sorry to ask you like this, Signor Pavani, but I was wondering whether you might have some work for me so that I can help pay for Nonna's treatment?'

Aldo Pavani took a moment and stroked his bearded chin. 'I have known Maria many years. Tell her I will come and visit her soon. It so happens Emi that I am looking for young, fit workers for the summer. Come and see me at the farm in the morning and we'll see what we can do.'

Emi was delighted with the opportunity he now faced as he set out early the next morning and headed for the farm. He had decided not to say anything to Nonna until work was secured. When he arrived at the farm, Signor Pavani took him into the kitchen of the farmhouse, offered him coffee and they sat together at the large table in the centre of the room. The table at one end was untidily covered with papers.

Signor Pavani waved his hand at the pile of documents, 'I am a farmer, not a clerk, but this is the way of things at present.' After a long sigh he continued, 'Emi, I have taken on three young men from town for the summer, but I can find work for a fourth if you would like that? It will be hard work, but I am sure you will be up to it.'

'I am very grateful to you. I will work very hard for you and do whatever you ask of me.'

'There is just one condition Emi. The authorities are telling me that I must employ only those who have signed up to membership of the Fascist Party. The three youths I am taking on have each applied to join the *Avanguardia Giovanile Fascista*.' As he placed a piece of paper in front of Emi, he said 'I have tried to help by completing this form for you. All it needs is your signature.'

Emi was stunned and did not know what to say. He froze. He desperately wanted the work, but all he had learnt of the Fascist Party from Leonardo had left him revulsed. He had long since resolved never to support the Fascist movement.

There was no mistaking the look on his face. Aldo Pavani sighed. 'It's just a means to an end Emi. Just sign and let's get to work.'

'You have been very kind to offer me work, Signor Pavani, but is there no other way? I do not want to get you into trouble with the authorities, but I really cannot sign.'

Aldo Pavani was silent for a few moments. He took the unsigned document back from Emi. 'I want to help you and

Maria if I can. Be here early on Monday and we'll put you to work.'

Emi was still expressing his gratitude as he exited the farmhouse into the yard and headed home.

Nonna smiled anxiously when she learnt Emi had found work to help her. She gave him a hug and kissed his forehead. Leonardo glowed with pride when, later that day, Emi told him what he had not told Nonna.

FOUR

Emi worked hard over the summer. He toiled in the fields from dawn to dusk and during those weeks he sorely missed his daily visits to Leonardo and the *biblioteca*. His good work impressed Aldo Pavani and he offered to keep him on for the harvest. Emi was short of the funds he needed for Nonna's consultation and he jumped at the opportunity.

By the end of October, his work was done. Aldo Pavani thanked him and encouraged him to return the following summer. The money Emi received was barely enough, but as soon as it was possible arrangements were made for Nonna to travel to Bologna. She was weak and needed the support of both Emi and Leonardo for the journey.

As they travelled home, Nonna reassured her anxious supporters that the doctor had been very positive. He had given her some new medication and had told her to rest.

Emi continued to divide his week between helping Nonna at home and, when able, snatching time at the *biblioteca* with Leonardo and Luca. As they arrived at Leonardo's home one morning in November, they found him as they had never seen him before. His mood was black and his palpable anger left him initially speechless. Emi was hesitant, unsure how to react at first. Even Luca delayed before quietly edging to the kitchen to find his morning pasta.

Leonardo sat slumped in a chair. He seemed distant, until Luca pushed his forehead into Leonardo's dangling hand. He stroked him gently before looking at Emi. 'He's done it Emi; he's got his way and our country will be ruined.'

Leonardo explained that Baron Giacomo Acerbo had successfully secured his proposals for electoral change meaning that in a future election the party with the largest share of the vote, as long as that share was as little as twenty five percent, would automatically be awarded two thirds of the seats in parliament. Leonardo had little doubt that an election would now soon be called.

Leonardo's mood was infectious and Emi began to feel that his world was changing for the worse; it was out of control and uncertainty hung over them like a heavy black storm cloud. He tried to remain positive when with Nonna, but she was not showing the signs of improvement in her health that she assured him the doctor had promised.

Sure enough, in April 1924 elections were held. There was widespread Fascist intimidation of voters and the Fascist group 'secured' sixty four percent of the vote. The opposition parties had won a majority of the votes in the north and the leader of the reformist socialists, Giacomo Matteotti, denounced Fascist violence and the election result.

On 10 June 1924, Matteotti disappeared. His body was found weeks later. There were arrests of Fascists who were linked with the murder, but, although only a handful of convictions were achieved, they were swiftly followed by the King's amnesty.

—※—

Nonna died peacefully in her sleep on 7 November 1924. Emi was filled with a sadness he had never felt before; not even when his father had died. At first he could not explain, however, why there was a part of him that felt ready to deal with both his sadness and the road ahead, but on reflection, he could see that both Nonna and Leonardo had been preparing him for this day. He suspected that Nonna had told Leonardo more about her condition than she had shared with Emi. As she became increasingly bed bound, Leonardo and Emi had taken turns to read to her in the evenings and there were a couple of occasions when Emi stumbled across them talking with a book laid flat on Leonardo's lap, only for his reading to resume as soon as Emi appeared.

Nonna's funeral was a simple event at the cemetery in Bardi. She was known to so many in the area and the attendance at her farewell reflected this. There were flowers and loving messages from her children and their families in America who were unable to afford the cost of travel at the time, but Zio Agostino arrived from Wales the day before the funeral.

Agostino was a big man of forty years. His jet black hair showed the early signs of silver edging, but his moustache retained its ebony colour, waxed and curled at the ends into a shape that Emi had never seen before on a human face.

Neither had he previously heard Italian spoken with the accent that emanated from his uncle's deep voice. The lyrical tone was unmistakably Italian, but there was a warm lilt that Emi could not place.

They greeted each other with an affectionate kiss to each cheek, but Agostino retained a firm grip on his nephew's shoulders as he backed away, looked sadly into his eyes and then smiled slightly as he pulled him close and gave him a huge bear hug.

The day after the funeral, Emi and Agostino were sat at Nonna's kitchen table. 'I can see how difficult things have been for you Emi. I wish I could have done more to help. Mamma and I wrote to each other regularly, but she did not tell me she was so unwell.'

'She did not tell me the whole story either, Zio.'

'A few months ago, she wrote to me about you. She loved you dearly Emi and wanted to communicate with me about your future. She wrote as if she was planning for the distant future and did not tell me that her health was so poor, but I can see now she was preparing me for this conversation with you today. She wrote about your love of this town and the surrounding countryside, about the people you love and respect nearby, but she could also see the changes that were coming and that you, too, had begun to express your fears for this country. Emi, you are sixteen and you are old enough to make a decision of your own, but Mamma and I concluded that when the time came, I would offer you the chance to come with me to live in Britain.'

Agostino could see the look of surprise in Emi's eyes. He had not expected his uncle to suggest this and thought he might instead talk about ways in which he would help him remain at home.

'Emi, I realise how big a step this would be for you. I cannot promise you it will be easy. I remember when I left here for a new life and how anxious I was about what I would find; but I promise you, aside from leaving Mamma, I did not regret it one bit. You can be with your family in Wales; we will all welcome you with open arms. I can offer you work. A new life away from the black disease that is gradually seeping into every corner of this country.'

Emi's head was spinning. After a while he was able to say 'Thank you Zio. I need some time to think. Would that be alright?'

'Of course Emi. Take your time; ask me any questions you like. I need to stay for a little while to finalise Mamma's affairs. I would be aiming to head home in the third week of December; I hope you will come with me, but I will help you whatever you decide.'

The next day, Emi and Luca took a long walk in the hills as Emi tried to resolve the wildly conflicting thoughts that were racing through his mind. It was bitterly cold, but somehow that helped him think.

Late in the afternoon he found himself unconsciously knocking on Leonardo's door. He could see straight away that Leonardo knew why he was there.

'Emi, I want you to know that I suggested to your grandmother you come and live with me when the time came. She knew she was very unwell, but she did not want to worry you. You are always welcome here, but she and I agreed that a life in Britain right now would give you the best chance of fulfilling your huge potential. It would be a great loss to this country – god knows it needs young men like you – but as things stand, the evil in this land will suffocate you and I cannot stand by and see that happen to my dear friend.'

Emi knew he was right. He fought back his tears and embraced Leonardo.

Plans were quickly made for their departure in the third week of December. They were to set off early and on the morning of the day before, Emi and Luca walked to Grezzo. It was cold, but sunny and crisp. Luca walked slowly this morning and stayed close to Emi's side as they wound through the trees.

Leonardo welcomed Emi in and sat him close to the fire. They drank coffee whilst Luca picked at his pasta. After a while Emi silently stood up and left the room. He walked slowly past the shelves of the *biblioteca*, touching as many of the spines as he could. At the end of the row he took a deep breath, trying to bury away a lasting memory of the heady smell of books and old wood and then returned to where Leonardo and Luca were now waiting for him at the rear door.

Leonardo embraced Emi and told him he would write for as long as foreign correspondence might be permitted. As Emi stood back, Leonardo handed him a small parcel wrapped in plain brown paper. 'Open it later,' he said.

Luca was sat silently next to Leonardo in the entrance to what he instinctively knew was his new home. Emi sank to his knees in front of Luca and took him in his arms. Luca licked his cheek and caught the tear that escaped the corner of his eye.

As their train headed out of Milan, Emi opened the brown paper parcel. It was the small book on fungi that they had looked at together the morning Emi had arrived with a truffle in his pocket – *'Funghi Nativi Italiani'*. Leonardo had written inside. *'For a worthy custodian. Forever your friends, Leonardo and Luca.'*

On 4 January 1925, Leonardo hurriedly wrote to Emi. It was a short letter to re-assure him that Luca was settling, as well as passing comment in terse terms about political developments, but it was written at speed for fear it might be some time before he could write about all but the plainest of subjects again.

The previous day, Mussolini had given a speech before the Chamber of Deputies. He feared a revolt within the party membership and so chose no longer to hide behind superficial words of democracy. Instead, he took responsibility for Fascist violence. Leonardo sensed that liberties were about to end and *il crotalo* was rising above the nation and hissing at those who dared look him in the eye.

Leonardo's letter ended *'You got out just in time my friend.'*

FIVE

Wales – 1925

Emi was fascinated by every detail of the journey to Britain. He had never before travelled outside Italy and whilst he and Agostino spoke at length at train stations waiting for connections, when on the train his attention was fixed on what he could see through the large windows, whilst often, Agostino drifted into sleep.

He was captivated by the alpine passes through which they wound and listened intently to the sounds of new languages at station stops where locomotives and guards were changed as they crossed in and out of Switzerland. The wide open landscapes alongside the French rail lines eventually gave way to larger towns and cities. Emi had been looking forward to the ferry crossing into Britain, but it was dark by the time they set sail and the sea was rough. He quickly discovered that, despite his Piscean birth, he was not a natural seafarer. As he raised his head for the umpteenth time from the toilet bowl, he swore never again to set foot on a ship.

Emi's lack of travel experience left him uninquiring about the formalities of entering Britain as a foreign national. It was all taken care of by his uncle who spoke to a uniformed man to whom he showed various documents. It all seemed very straight forward.

The journey from the coast to London was also in the dark and sleep eventually overtook him. When they found themselves finally at Paddington Station they had a long wait on cold benches for their morning train to the west.

It was on Paddington Station that Emi had his first experience of British coffee. His uncle handed him the steaming mug and stood watching Emi, intently waiting for his reaction. He laughed when his young nephew could not hide his disappointment. 'Don't worry Emi,' he laughed, patting one of the two large suitcases that sat beside their bench, 'I have returned with a taste of home.'

When they finally arrived at a Welsh station whose name Emi quickly decided he had no hope of pronouncing, they were met by a middle aged man who greeted Agostino and shook Emi's hand, introducing himself as William. He drove them north through heavy rain and it was not long before a large road sign announced their arrival in the village of Tumble.

Agostino had done his best to describe life in Tumble during their journey. As they entered the village and drove along the main road, Emi could see little more than a row of small terraced houses on each side, interspersed with a number of shops set back a little from the kerb. They slowed as they passed the café so that Agostino could point it out to Emi. He was able to make out red lettering which announced his uncle's name above a large glass window. Either side of his name, he thought he could make out a black shape which he realised was identical to the unmistakable curl of Agostino's moustache. It made him giggle and Agostino joined in when he realised the cause of his merriment.

They did not stop at the café, but instead turned off the road and pulled up in front of a small house painted white and green. As he stepped through the door, Emi was enveloped by the substantial embrace of Agostino's wife, Isabella.

After he was shown to his room and had a wash, Emi joined the family at the kitchen table for a simple meal. Isabella had already raided the enticing contents of Agostino's suitcases. They were joined by Emi's cousins, Paolo, who was twelve and Francesca, who was eight. They had been born in Wales and were at ease speaking in both the Italian and English languages. They were intrigued by Emi and quickly added to his exhaustion from the journey by bombarding him with questions, which Isabella tried to deflect by reminding them that there would be plenty of time for them to explore their curiosity in the days to come.

Agostino said that he would show Emi around the next day and take him to the café. In the meantime, Isabella encouraged him to get some sleep. Before he stood to head to bed, Francesca confidently told her mother that she would teach her cousin English. 'You can help, Fran, but let's leave it to Ella.'

The next morning, Agostino led Emi from the house and introduced him to everyone who crossed their path. The names were too many to retain at the time, but all those he met seemed welcoming and kind.

The distance to the café was not long, but they were slowed by their many encounters with villagers. When they eventually triggered the soft welcoming bell as they stepped through the café door, Emi found himself in a space filled with light walls and well made wooden tables and chairs. It was early, but many of the tables were already occupied by villagers eating breakfast or drinking coffee. At the back of the café there was a counter behind which a tall young man was stood, wearing a long striped apron. To his left was a long glass and chrome topped ice cream bar.

As they shut the door behind them, all the occupants of the café called out almost in unison welcoming the proprietor's return. '*Ciao* Gus' – 'Welcome home, Gus' – 'What took you so long Gus?' – 'The coffee's been terrible since you left' – the last said by a youth who grinned at the aproned man behind the counter.

Agostino stood before them, told them that he had missed most, but not all, of them and proceeded to introduce his nephew Emi, who would be bringing his 'authentic Italian culinary skills to the best café in the village.' He was quickly reminded by an elderly man in the corner that this was the *only* café in the village.

They walked through to the back of the café and Emi was introduced to the aproned Alberto. It was he who showed Emi the ropes over the next few days. He had been working at the café for the last year and lived with his wife and young children in the flat above. Before that he had been working for an Italian ice cream producer in Ebbw Vale where he learnt his craft and when Agostino decided to branch out into the business of *gelato*, Alberto answered the advertisement keen to move closer to his Welsh wife's family who were born and bred in Cross Hands.

Ice cream was never going to take over from the café's core business, but Agostino was pleased with how quickly it became popular. The children ate it as a treat whatever the weather, but, surprisingly, it also became a summer favourite of the miners and youths of the village who enjoyed the refreshment it gave in the heat of the day after the exertion of a shift or a game.

On the journey from Italy, Agostino had explained that Tumble had developed in the last century to house the miners who were employed at the nearby anthracite mines. The Great Mountain colliery had drifts that were some of the longest and deepest in the Gwendraeth Valley and by the time of Emi's arrival, the mine had a workforce of around a thousand. It was they who formed the core of the café's customers, calling in at all times of the day before and after shifts to re-fuel and to catch up with locals and friends before much needed sleep or heading out to the pit. Agostino joked that it was always possible to tell whether a miner was coming or going because, although a bath was the first port of call after a shift, it proved impossible to wash out the stubborn seams of dark coal dust deposited in the natural creases of the miners' faces and hands after a single wash.

Long opening hours were therefore maintained at the café to capture the rotating trade. It often did not close until

11 at night and was up and running with breakfasts as early as 5 in the morning.

Emi was quickly put to work in the kitchen and, with Alberto's help, he soon picked up the skills he needed to keep the customers well-fed, refreshed and happy. Without an ability to speak the language, however, he could help little at the counter and so within a week of arriving aunt Isabella was sat with Emi in her kitchen, introducing him to Gabriella Angharad di Costa.

'Welcome to hell,' were the first words that Ella said to Emi in perfect Italian, albeit with a strong Welsh accent, as she shook his hand.

The young woman who stood before him was about his age; perhaps a little younger. She had the thick dark hair, brown eyes and olive complexion that her Mediterranean heritage had gifted to her. She wore a large miner's jacket which was too long in the sleeves for her, thick trousers and heavy miner's boots tied up with yellow laces.

She inspected Emi briefly, before adding 'Isabella has asked me to teach you English. I'll meet you at the café tomorrow morning at 11.'

She turned and left.

Isabella could see the trepidation that crossed Emi's face. 'Don't worry, she's not as scary as she likes to think she is.'

His aunt explained that Ella was the daughter of a Welsh born miner whose own father had emigrated to Wales from Cremona. She had not long finished school and seemed to be going through a phase of 'hating' village life and, as Ella saw it, the male dominated atmosphere created by miners and rugby players.

'It's fair to say that Ella's view of the world is a work in progress; you can't always be sure from one day to the next what she's thinking at the moment,' Isabella explained. 'But what I can tell you is that she was born to teach. She has already spent a couple of weeks, when needed, at the local school where she could be seen at lunchtimes with half a dozen children hanging off the fingers of each hand. She is the first to be called if a translator is needed. She'll teach you well.'

Emi worked the next morning until 1055 and then, with Agostino's agreement, he sat quietly at a corner table awaiting Ella's arrival. It was clear to him that she would expect him to be on time. The soft bell of the opening door announced her arrival as if it were the striking of a clock, so precise was she with her timing. She wore the same miner's coat and boots from the previous day.

Ella sat opposite Emi and said 'Good morning,' in English. He had heard the phrase in the café enough to know what it meant and carefully, albeit brokenly, returned the greeting in English. Ella appeared pleased with his effort. Emi searched his mind to work out if he had picked up enough from the café's usual exchanges to continue in English, but after pursing his lips together he thought better of it, despite Ella's look of encouragement. Instead he asked her if she would like coffee – in Italian. Ella looked disappointed, but welcomed the offer – in English.

When he returned with the coffee he found Ella stood, placing her coat on the back of her chair. The oversized coat had hidden a slight young woman whose huge boots now looked even more incongruous. Emi found himself wondering whether they concealed equally dainty feet, or whether she was a very fast swimmer. Ella reached into the pocket of her coat and retrieved a book which she placed on the table in front of her as she re-took her seat.

Emi was relieved when Ella next spoke in Italian. 'Learning a new language takes commitment Emi. Are you ready to commit?'

He saw the steely look in Ella's eyes and he knew the only acceptable response could be 'I am.'

'Good. The only way to do this is to meet regularly and for you to use the language, however badly at first. We will meet twice each day, including Saturdays. I suggest here at 11 in the morning and then at 6 in the evening. I have already cleared this with Gus – you can have an hour away from work twice a day until you have learnt enough to speak to customers and then we'll take stock. We'll get away from this table as much as possible and explore the outdoors and the words that go with it, but success will depend on you doing some studying in your own time.' As she said this, she pushed the book before her across the table to Emi.

The book was entitled *'English Grammar'*. It was in English which left Emi perplexed. 'I know,' Ella said, 'but once you have learnt the basics from me you will find this book helpful.'

Emi opened the front cover. Inside a stamp asserted in firm terms that the book was school property. Even though her pupil did not yet understand the meaning of those words, Ella looked sheepish as she felt the need to explain,

'I'm just looking after it.' After a moment she added 'Right, let's go – get your coat.'

They headed out into the street and slowly along the main road. As they walked Ella gave Emi the English name of multiple objects they passed. She encouraged him to repeat the word after her and told him not to worry too much about remembering every word at this stage. They passed the Tumble Hall and the Baptist Chapel and headed uphill towards the edge of the village. When they got to the village name sign, they turned to head back.

Emi expressed curiosity about the village name. 'Do you know what the English word "Tumble" means?' asked Ella. When he confirmed he did not, she explained 'To tumble – *"ruzzolare"* or *"capitombolare"*.' Emi politely suggested this was an odd name for a village. Ella agreed; she thought it originated from the name of the inn that stood nearby when the village was built in the last century.

'We'll need a separate lesson for Welsh place names Emi,' said Ella. 'I'm teaching you English, not Welsh, but you'll need to get used to pronunciations and some words that carry a Welsh language influence or the Welsh word itself.'

Emi's shoulders sank a little. 'Do I need to learn *two* languages?'

Ella laughed, 'One step at a time. Almost everyone here speaks English and Welsh, but certainly everyone understands English. There are one or two villagers who will *only* use the Welsh language in reply, but you'll get used to it. You'll have seen Dai Evans sat in the corner of the café each morning making a cup of tea last hours. He's a good and proud Welshman, but watch out, he'll run rings round you if you're not careful. Maybe I can teach you a little Welsh too; let's see how it goes. "Tumble" in Welsh, for example, is *"Y Tymbl".'*

Ella pulled out a pencil and a piece of paper from her voluminous jacket pocket. She wrote the word *'Llanelli'* and asked Emi to read it out loud. He hesitated and then softly rolled the 'l's' as in 'Ella'. She gave him the correct pronunciation and slowly, Emi repeated it.

With a smile Ella said 'You'll need to get to know the local towns and villages; you'll need to know your Tumbles from your Mumbles.' When she saw the quizzical look on Emi's face she added 'To mumble – *"borbottare".'*

Now Emi looked exasperated, 'There is also a place called Mumble?'

Ella laughed at Emi's bemusement. 'There is. Mumbles. Actually, my mother is from Swansea and she tells me the name does not come from the English word, but rather from the French word *"mamelles"*, which describes the shape of the headland. Do you know what that means?'

Emi hesitated awkwardly. The French word was close enough to the Italian for him to need no translation. If it was Ella's intention to embarrass him by tricking him into saying the word 'breasts' in any language in her presence, he was not going to fall for it. 'I do,' he simply replied; then added 'Let's head back, it's getting cold.' Ella laughed and followed him down the hill.

S I X

In the weeks that followed, Emi found himself happily occupied with work in the café and language lessons with Ella. Alberto was clearly relieved to have Emi's help and his presence enabled him to spend more time with his young family, for which he was very grateful. Gus made regular trips to Bristol to visit his own uncle who had moved there from Wales several years before to open a new restaurant and sometimes he and his uncle travelled to London, meeting with a group of Italian business men who tried to provide support and finance for compatriots who had fallen on hard times.

Thus, there were some occasions when Emi was left running the café alone. Isabella tried to be on hand as much as possible during those times, but she was rarely available outside school hours when she was busy caring for Paolo and Francesca. Emi enjoyed the responsibility. His English was developing fast and Ella told him she was 'very impressed.' He had even begun to get to grips with the text on grammar.

When running the café alone, he could not sit with Ella for his twice daily lessons, but that did not stop her. When she knew he was alone, she spent much of the day at the café with Emi engaging him between customers in English and frequently coming behind the counter to help him when it was busy.

One morning in early March, Emi found himself alone at the café waiting for Ella to join him. Isabella came in and told him she had a message from Ella that she could not come in today because the school needed her help to fill in for a teacher absent through illness. He assured Isabella that he would be fine running the café alone – it was unusually quiet and Emi suspected that a circulating flu bug had something to do with that.

When Isabella left, the only customer was Dai sat in his usual corner seat nursing a cold cup of tea. As the door shut behind Isabella, Dai lifted his gaze from the bottom of his cup and looked Emi square in the eye.

The first time Dai had approached Emi in the café, he ordered his cup of tea in Welsh. Emi was well prepared. Not only had Ella forewarned him, but she had also painstakingly taught him single Welsh words which were likely regularly to pass Dai's lips. In truth, Dai never ordered anything other than a cup of tea, so whilst pronunciation was largely still beyond Emi, he knew he could recognise '*paned o de*' if Dai dropped that on him. On that first order, Emi smiled, span away from the counter and made Dai's tea. When he handed it to him, Dai's disappointment that he had not caught Emi out was written all over his face.

Now, Dai had got him alone. His eyes narrowed and he

held Emi's gaze as he rose from his table. He approached the counter slowly with the deliberate step of a gunslinger and suddenly Emi regretted his confidence in his ability to run the café alone that morning.

Emi focused on Dai's lips as he spoke, but he heard no sound; panic had closed his ears. When his blank look led to a grin and repetition from Dai, Emi's brain turned the volume back up, but the words meant nothing to him. He refused to give in. What could Dai be saying? Emi decided that any response was better than nothing, so he turned on his heel, made a plate of bacon and eggs and, whilst avoiding Dai's gaze, placed it on the counter. When he finally dared look Dai in the eye again, he expected to see a look of triumph, but instead he was crestfallen. Dai picked up his plate and shuffled back to his table.

Emi stood at the counter for a while, wondering whether he should take up poker, but then turned, made a fresh cup of tea and walked over to Dai. He gestured to the cup already on the table and in an attempt to point out that it was cold said '*awful*'. Dai grinned and corrected him: 'O*erfel.*' Dai reached into his pocket, but Emi held up his hand to stop him and took the cold cup of tea away.

With a fresh cup, Dai merely extended his long silent stay until lunchtime. Suddenly Emi realised how much he missed Ella's company. At half past one, Dai rose to his feet and headed for the door. Before he closed it behind him, he looked over at Emi and called '*Grazie* Emi.'

When Emi told Ella about his stand off with Dai, she laughed uncontrollably and punched him in the arm with glee. 'You know, it's said Dai was a wily player in his day, but you side stepped his tackle and headed for the try line didn't you.'

The confusion on Emi's face led to their first conversation about rugby. It was still a relatively new sport in Italy and he knew little about it. Although it was quickly clear that Ella had a detailed knowledge of the game, it was equally clear that she held the locals who played it in low esteem. 'Most of them are a bunch of fools who spend half their time assaulting each other on the pitch and the other half drunk.'

They were walking through the village as Ella administered her daily high speed vocabulary test, insisting that Emi provide the English word for twenty items she pointed to in rapid succession. His score stood at 14/14 when she decided to try and catch him out by pointing to the floor as they negotiated a corner. He turned his gaze to look in the direction of Ella's gesture and found himself still trying to work out whether she was pointing to the large dog turd in the gutter as he walked head first into an immovable object.

Embarrassment that he had probably made a fool of himself in front of Ella by walking into a lamp post was quickly replaced by disbelief when he saw that his head had collided with the broad chest of a giant.

'I am sorry,' the giant said as he placed a huge hand on Emi's shoulder to stop him falling backwards, 'I didn't see you there.'

'Honestly Bryn,' exclaimed Ella, 'can't you see us poor Lilliputians down here? Be careful. Are you alright Emi?'

Before Emi stood a young man, perhaps a few years older than himself, but twice the size. He wore a miner's jacket and his face was covered in coal dust.

'Oh, it's you Ella. How is my favourite cousin today? Haven't seen you for a while. Where have you been hiding?' Without waiting for an answer, Bryn turned to her companion. 'Emi, is it? Good to meet you. Sorry we haven't met sooner, but welcome to Tumble.'

As Emi tried politely to withdraw his blackened hand from the vice like handshake Bryn had offered, he addressed Bryn in the formal English language version that represented the limit of his 'greeting' knowledge thus far.

Bryn grinned. 'I see Ella is teaching you well. Everyone tells me you're *devoted* to your task Ella!'

Ella looked embarrassed and kicked her cousin's shin. He appeared to feel no pain.

'Got to go,' said Bryn. 'It's been a long shift and I need a bath. I'll come see you at the café Emi. That is if Ella gives you time off for good behaviour.'

As he set off Ella scowled at the back of her cousin's head. He raised a hand behind him, waving without turning. She remained quiet for a while as they continued their walk and so Emi asked 'Bryn is your cousin?'

'Yes, he's the son of my mother's sister. We grew up together. He works hard at the mine with his father, but I'm afraid, like so many of the miners, he too has fallen into the company of those rugby bores. Given the size of him, it was only a matter of time before coach Carwyn lured him into the team. Carwyn boasts it usually takes four of the opposition to floor Bryn and now he has his eyes set on success for the club. To be fair, Bryn is a big softy under that huge exterior.' Ella paused before continuing, 'I just wish he wouldn't spend so much time with those fools.'

At the café, when there were quiet moments, Emi had taken to reading newspapers left behind by customers. It helped the development of his language skills and was encouraged by Ella, but he also welcomed the opportunity to find out what was happening in the world and was keen to pick out any news of his homeland. There had been a couple of occasions when Gus had returned from meetings in London laden with Italian ingredients and sometimes he had managed to get hold of an Italian newspaper which he gave to Emi.

Leonardo wrote from time to time, but it was clear he felt increasingly constrained in what he could say. His last letter re-assured Emi that he and Luca were well, but '*our walks are closer to home at present as it is so easy these days to stumble upon a snake.*' Emi was in no doubt as to Leonardo's meaning. He wrote back when he could, but kept his letters short for fear he might say the wrong thing and get his friend into some kind of difficulty.

It was a couple of weeks after their first meeting when Bryn Williams, true to his word, squeezed through the door of the café mid morning as Emi stood at the counter, his head down, wrestling with some new words in a copy of yesterday's news.

'Good morning Emi. How are you?' he asked with a broad grin, his coal dust free features visible to Emi for the first time. 'I thought I would pop in for a chat and the other half of my breakfast.'

Emi greeted Bryn warmly and hesitatingly asked, 'Er… you want half a breakfast?'

Bryn laughed. 'Oh no, a full breakfast please Emi, anything less would not do the job. Mam always cooks my breakfast first thing, but by eleven I'm a bit peckish so she cooks me the "other half". She tells me I'm still a "growing lad". That's all well and good, but when she goes off to town as she has today, I risk stunting my growth unless I can find someone to step in.'

'So you have two full breakfasts every day?' Emi asked.

'Alright Emi, don't rub it in. It takes a lot of fuel to keep the firebox in this fine-tuned machine fully stoked you know.'

Business was in a brief mid-morning lull and so they chatted as Emi prepared Bryn's breakfast.

'So, how are you settling in Emi?' Bryn asked.

'I feel very welcome here Bryn. Gus and his family have been very kind to me.'

'He's a good man. Heart of gold.'

Bryn ate the other half of his breakfast in silence clearly unable to hold a conversation whilst he shovelled fuel into his mouth, as if worried he would run out of steam if the rate of supply dropped below a well practised pace.

'So are you a sportsman Emi?' Bryn eventually asked as he put down his knife and fork on an empty plate.

'Not really Bryn. I used to think I could run fast, but I only ever really ran when I was late for something. My favourite thing is to read. I do most of that sitting down.'

Bryn's eyes lit up at the word 'fast' and he did not seem to hear any of the other words that followed it. 'Now Emi it so happens that coach Carwyn is looking for a left wing. Do you fancy a game of rugby?'

Emi did not respond. What was he to say? He liked Bryn and part of him really wanted to get involved with the rugby scene and meet new people, but he could not help but hear Ella's voice in his ear and he was in no doubt she would disapprove if he became involved with 'those fools'.

It was not difficult for Bryn to recognise what was going through Emi's mind. 'Listen, you don't need to worry about Ella. She just thinks most men are a bore. It's a phase I'm sure. Her father played for the club until he broke his leg in a match and up 'til that point she used to stand on the touchline cheering us on. Look, you won't know if it's the game for you until you give it a go. It's a game for all shapes and sizes. Why don't you come to training one evening and see what you think? Ella doesn't need to know.'

Emi heard himself agreeing an instant before the sound of the slap of delight Bryn landed on his back.

SEVEN

A few days later, Emi found himself arriving with Bryn at a training session at the club ground. He was greeted by a stocky man in his thirties who held out his hand to Emi and introduced himself as the coach, Carwyn Bennett. He was clearly expected. 'Welcome Emiliano. I hear you're fast – just what we need. Why don't you head into the clubhouse there; we've found you some kit which should fit for now. The boots may be a little big, but hopefully they won't slow you down too much.'

Bryn had already told Emi that Carwyn had taken over the coaching role at the club some six months earlier and had set about turning the team into a 'winning side'. Away from the rugby world, he was the village police sergeant and well known to the locals. 'He's a good coach Emi,' Bryn had told him, 'but he can be a bit strict when he's unhappy with what he sees. He says he is going to "change the culture" here; better diet, less drinking. "Moderation in all things" is the principle we must live by, he says. He's going to turn us into "well-oiled machines". Trouble is

Emi, some of us still prefer the lubrication on offer across the bar after a match.'

Bryn introduced Emi to some of the other players. True to Bryn's words they appeared to be of all shapes and sizes. Short, tall, thin, large, all in a variety of combinations. And then there was Bryn: a size and shape all of his own.

The coach had two others on his staff. 'William the Taxi' who had met Emi at the train station the first night he arrived in Wales and 'PC Dafydd' an enthusiastic teenager. William Edwards was not a taxi driver and Dafydd Bennett was not a police constable. William was a locksmith who had inherited the biggest car in the village from his father; he was happy to be called on when transport was needed. Dafydd was Carwyn's nephew, obsessed with the idea of becoming a policeman. Carwyn had doubts about the supply of common sense god had given his nephew and tried gently to discourage his fixation by nurturing new interests. At the club, he did all sorts of odd jobs as the need arose, but many of the players just found him irritating and bit their tongues only to avoid falling foul of their coach.

Emi did not know what to expect as he emerged onto the pitch. He knew nothing of the rules of the game and he was caught unawares when immediately coach Carwyn shouted 'catch' as he launched a ball off his foot high into the air. Emi looked up and tried to work out the ball's trajectory as it began to fall out of orbit, but the stiff breeze took the ball away from him at the last moment and his inept one handed lunge left him feeling embarrassed.

For the next twenty minutes the entire group ran around the pitch; slowly along each end next to the posts and sprinting along each length. Emi was taken aback by the speed of some of the larger players, but he was able to hold his own and as the session went on he found that he was pulling away from the rest at the end of each length.

Passing and kicking sessions followed. Emi struggled. He could not help but think the inventor of this game had been intoxicated when coming up with the shape of the ball. Tackling practice left him bruised. Coach Carwyn showed Emi how to get low and avoid a head injury, but as Alun Edwards, who was of the short but large variety, charged towards Emi he found the shape of the player as awkward as he had found the shape of the ball and ended up flat on his back after Alun's boot connected with his right eye.

Coach Carwyn thought that was enough for a first session for Emi, but he stayed at the ground to watch the players in the thirty minute game which rounded off the training session and began to get a sense of the structure of the game, whilst remaining largely bemused by the rules.

As he left, coach Carwyn said he looked forward to seeing Emi at training next week. There did not seem to be any thought for the possibility that this game was not perhaps for him and Emi felt some pleasure in the apparent endorsement of his potential.

Emi wiped the bathroom mirror as he looked into it the following morning, in an attempt to remove the mark appearing through the steamed up glass, the latter a product of the hot water Isabella had poured into the sink for him just before he rose out of bed. A second unsuccessful wipe brought the realisation that he was sporting the deep purple phase of an angry black eye.

He had already been in no doubt that word would get back to Ella somehow that he had been at the rugby club; despite Bryn's assurances Emi was aware that nothing in the village got past her. Now, the as yet unresolved calculation of what best, if anything, to say to her required a time critical solution; in a few hours he would be face to face with the disapproving stare of his teacher.

By the time he got to the café he had accepted that short of finding something in the fridge that would perfectly match his skin tone, honesty was the only option. He could not meet her gaze as Ella walked through the door. She joined him at the table where he had already placed her coffee. Emi wondered whether she would show some concern for him, thinking on first glance perhaps that he had befallen some accident, but when he felt brave enough to look at her it was apparent that she already knew everything.

Ella took a deep breath. 'Today we are going to work on some grammar.' After a pause she added frostily, 'And *only* grammar.'

'I'm sorry Ella,' Emi said after a while.

'Emi, you have no reason to apologise to me. You do as you wish. Bryn came round early this morning. He's seen enough eye injuries to know your face would tell its own story today. He told me not to be hard on you; it was all his fault. I told him there was no reason to explain any of this to me. It matters not to me what you do Emi. I don't know why he thinks I should be surprised by the foolish things men do. Now, let's get on with your lesson.'

Ella's coffee was left untouched, gradually becoming as cold as her demeanour throughout the following hour. When his time was up she said 'I think we are pretty much at the point where you know enough English now to deal with most things at the café. That was what we agreed we would aim for so I think I'll let Gus know.'

Emi tried to protest saying he did not feel confident yet that he knew enough. He even expressed his objection in a calculated broken English in the hope his incompetence would be self evident, but Ella was not fooled. She rose from her seat, said a polite farewell and headed for the door. Emi called out to Ella before the door shut behind her, but she either did not hear him or chose to ignore him.

The following day, Ella did not arrive for their lesson.

———

For two days Emi's head was full of regret and hopeless ideas for mending the damage he felt he had done. On the morning of day three, a Saturday, he woke in an indignant mood. All he had done was go to a training session with a group of likeable lads and play around with an odd shaped leather ball. What was Ella's problem with that?

His mood had not changed when Bryn walked into the café first thing. Bryn had kept out of the way for a few days, not sure whether his decision to speak to Ella without consulting Emi had made things better or worse. He apologised to Emi who told him not to worry. 'She was always going to find out somehow Bryn. It's none of her business anyway.'

Bryn raised an eyebrow at that last remark and saw his chance to tell Emi why he had called in. 'I'm here Emi at the request of the coach. We've got a friendly match this afternoon with Pontyberem. It's been arranged to give both sides a run out, but we need a left wing as it's such short notice. Coach wondered if you'd like to give it a go?'

Emi had come away from that first training session unsure whether rugby was for him and lacking any confidence that he really understood the laws of the game. But the morning's mood was still running through his veins when he immediately said 'Yes.'

———

When Emi stepped onto the pitch in the black and white hoops of the team, he quickly realised that his bravado was still back at the café sipping coffee and laughing at the thought of what lay in wait for the young Italian flier.

For most of the first ten minutes of the game Emi was on the end of a stream of calls from his team mates to 'stay on side.' He stuck obediently to the left touchline and found himself getting cold as the ball seemed perpetually to be buried in the depths of a swarm of wrestling forwards.

Eventually the ball popped out from the forwards on their side and in a flash it was passed along the line of players towards him. Emi ran hard to keep up with the play and suddenly the ball was arcing into his chest where he just managed to hold onto it. He set off down the touchline as fast as he could, from thirty yards or so outside the opposition try line. It wasn't long before he became aware of the growing silhouette of Pontyberem's full back heading straight for him. What does he do now? Keep running? The closing speed of his opponent gave him no time to think. Just as they collided Emi felt an arm encircle his waist from behind and an injection of power that took him by surprise. Bryn was driving him through the opposition player towards the line. Emi held onto the ball as tightly as he could and out of the corner of his eye saw a cluster of unfriendly forwards heading towards them. Their impact took Emi off his feet and suddenly he was face down in the dirt under a pile of bodies.

Emi lay still while the boulders above him slowly rolled away and eventually he was able to fill his squashed lungs. He was still prone in the grass when he felt himself being lifted by his collar from behind. He heard Bryn's voice behind him as he planted Emi onto his feet saying 'nice try Emi' and then saw the shock on his face as Emi turned to him and revealed a nose at a most unnatural angle, smeared with blood and mud and sprinkled with a few blades of grass.

William the Taxi drove Emi to the local doctor who stood on no ceremony in grasping his patient's distorted nose and in one movement producing a *crack* that entered Emi's ears and reverberated down his spine. The doctor professed himself happy with the result, but warned Emi that once the swelling goes down 'You may find the alignment is not exactly as you remember it.'

So brief was the procedure that Emi was back pitch side when his team walked off as the victors of the day's battle. Bryn was pleased to see him and told him his injury would add a much needed rugged quality to his features – 'The young ladies of the village will be fighting for your attention.'

Most of the team intended to celebrate their win at the local pub and Emi took little persuasion to join them intent on drowning his sorrows. Coach Carwyn had long since decided that it was his duty to accompany the team on such occasions as the most effective means of trying to keep the consumption of beer to a reasonable level. His cry of 'moderation in all things now lads,' as they spilled into the bar, however, was always accepted as a challenge by the landlord who strongly disapproved of any instructions that might threaten the prospects for a profitable night.

It wasn't long before Carwyn could see he was fighting a losing battle. He sat a little morosely nursing his first pint, until Bryn placed a huge arm around his shoulders and shared some alcohol tinged logic with his coach. 'You know coach, "moderation in *all* things" must mean that we're required to indulge in a moderate amount of excess. Don't you think?' Carwyn's face slowly broke into a grin.

Everyone got very drunk.

⸺

The face that looked back at Emi through swollen eyes in the bathroom mirror the next morning was not his own. It was a horror show. His black eye had not gone away, but it was now barely visible behind his broad swollen nose and the purple panorama that stretched across his face, as if he were wearing a colourful silk blindfold. It was painful to the touch, but that morning he could not distinguish between the pain of his injuries and the throbbing hangover playing kettle drums inside his head. Dear god, he thought, what was he doing to himself?

For the next couple of days, while the swelling started to subside, Emi did a lot of thinking. When he had finished thinking he spoke to Gus who did not hesitate in agreeing to his nephew's plan for the following day.

At 10pm the next night, Emi shut the door of the café behind his last customer and turned the hanging sign to read '*closed*'. He removed the temporary sign next to it which he had placed there early that morning apologising that the café would close an hour early today.

Now he was alone, Emi swung into action. He lowered the café's blinds and raced to the kitchen area behind the counter where he had been preparing the ingredients for the meal he must now complete in the thirty minutes left to him.

The evening before, he had pushed an envelope through Ella's door. Inside was a short note inviting her to dinner at 1030pm. 'I wanted to find a way to thank you for teaching me English,' he wrote. 'I hope you will come.'

He had no way of knowing whether Ella would arrive, but Gus did what he could to remove any last minute hurdles and had a quiet word with Ella's parents to ensure they would not be concerned about their daughter being out late. 'Emi will be certain to get her home safely.'

Emi consulted Nonna's cookery book and Gus gave him free rein, 'Within reason please Emi,' to explore his pantry where he kept the Italian culinary treasures he secured from time to time. Pasta, garlic, tomatoes and a little *pecorino romano* found their way into Emi's bag. He visited the butcher and bought a little pork and some gelatine and from the café's fridge he collected some berries normally used to flavour the ice cream.

By 1025pm Emi was ready. He sat at the corner table they had always used for lessons, now laid out for dinner on a red and white gingham table cloth. He sat staring at the door. He knew that if Ella was coming she would be there at 1030 sharp. If she was not there by 1031, he may as well start clearing up.

The door opened only a little at first and Ella peered in as if uncertain whether anyone would actually be there. Emi sprang to his feet and opened the door the rest of the way. Ella stood before him in her miner's jacket.

'Come in,' Emi said. As he shut the door behind her, he noticed that in place of her trademark boots, Ella wore flat brown shoes. He found himself a little relieved that her feet were half the size he sometimes imagined them to be.

'I wasn't sure if you would come,' he said.

'Neither was I,' Ella replied looking nervously at her feet. She held the lapels of her jacket self consciously and felt the need to explain, 'My mother wanted me to wear my best coat, but that would feel like I had made my mind up to come here. This jacket gives me the choice to turn around at any point and take a walk in the night's cold air instead.'

Emi did not miss Ella's calculated use of the present tense. He knew she was making it clear that even though she had now arrived, she was still reserving the option to walk out.

'I'm glad you're here,' Emi said. 'Let me take your coat.'

As he moved towards her, Ella met his gaze for the first time since stepping through the door and her sudden intake of breath signalled to Emi that she could now see the full damage done to his face, even though it had begun its healing phase. She was unable to hide the slight slump of disappointment in her shoulders.

'I'm sorry about this,' Emi said, gesturing with his hand towards his face. 'I thought of softening the blow by using candle light tonight, but I'm afraid it makes me look like a ghoul. I tried it out on my cousins, but Francesca screamed and Paolo laughed; neither reaction was what I was hoping for tonight.'

Ella smiled and turned to allow Emi to remove her jacket. The elegant green dress beneath was not what he was expecting. 'You know it's rude to stare Emi,' Ella said after an awkward pause.

'Sorry. Let's eat.'

Emi seated Ella at their table, disappeared to the back of the café and was quickly back with plates of pasta. 'It smells wonderful,' said Ella.

As they began to eat, he told Ella that he wished he had a truffle to grate on the top and then found himself telling her all about the day of his find, about Luca and about his friendship with Leonardo.

After the diners had wiped their plates clean with bread, Emi removed them to the kitchen and returned with two set *latte inglese* covered in berries and their juices.

'You're a good cook, Emi. Thank you,' Ella announced as she placed her spoon on an empty plate and settled back into her chair. She looked more carefully at Emi's injuries and asked 'Does it hurt?'

'Not really. It looks worse than it is.'

Ella leaned forward and touched the top of Emi's nose gently. She ran her finger slowly down the new contour which now ended with a slight deviation to the southwest.

She sat back and said 'Emi, I'm sorry I was angry with you. My father used to play rugby and I enjoyed watching him. He broke his leg in a match and he could not work for three months; that was difficult for all of us – we had no other income. It all seemed a bit stupid to me; to cause serious injury and lose so much for the sake of a game. He still has a bit of limp, but it's done nothing to change his love of rugby. I know he still goes to the ground sometimes to watch matches. Honestly, Emi, if you want to play, play. There's no reason why you should let me change your mind.'

'I went to the station today and saw Carwyn,' Emi announced. 'I told him I won't be playing anymore.' He saw the look of both relief and guilt in Ella's expression and hastily added, 'It has nothing to do with your views mind Ella. I wanted to give it a go, but it's just not for me. Look at me!'

They both began to laugh.

'Carwyn tells me it's just a case of learning not to put my face in the wrong place. He says it's rare for someone to have so many injuries. Clearly, I am that rare case.' Emi continued after a pause, 'But I do like the game Ella. I like the people too. Even PC Dafydd doesn't irritate me *all* the time.'

Ella giggled.

'Ella, I want to go and watch a game now and again and support the boys.' He saw no reaction from her. 'I'll probably have a drink or two with them too.' Still no reaction; or was that a slight pursing of the lips? 'Do you think you'd like to come and watch a game with me some time?'

'I'll think about it.'

E I G H T

In the early summer of 1925 Emi began spending Sunday mornings at the café, when it was closed, with Alberto. They could both usually be found, dressed in the new short white coats Gus had purchased for use at the ice cream counter, carefully and slowly turning the contents of a pot or sat opposite each other tasting off spoons and making notes in a folder they had jokingly labelled on the cover '*la scienza del gelato e minatori*' – '*the science of ice cream and miners*'.

What began as a session with Alberto in which he taught Emi the basics of ice cream making, had soon turned into a joint obsession. Although the ice cream was selling well, they had decided to try and educate local tastebuds and persuade the mining community in their belief that low butter fat *gelato* was much the tastier option.

They had calculated the benefits of sourcing the larger quantities of milk, rather than cream, they needed from a local farm. They hoped to invest in a hand cranked churn, but for now they stirred the ingredients slowly and lovingly by hand in a pot surrounded by crushed ice off a block collected from the train up from Llanelli. They had persuaded Gus to let them experiment despite his concern that it may alienate the miners who were the primary purchasers of the ice cream they currently produced. Alberto and Emi were convinced the *gelato* would sell well if they could introduce some new varieties and it was flavour experiments upon which they were now mostly focussing. Gus reserved the right to taste the results of their labours in the 'laboratory' before giving any kind of go ahead.

Alberto's wife had only reluctantly agreed to this Sunday morning project, but strictly on the basis that he was back upstairs in the flat with his family by lunchtime. When Alberto departed, Emi usually remained tasting their morning's work whilst reading any newspapers left by Saturday's customers which he had collected and set aside. After an hour he would meet Ella and they would go for a walk, before both returning to the café where he tried the day's new flavours on her discerning palate.

Emi had hoped the almond flavour would win approval, but in the end it was the new blend of berry flavours that convinced Gus to give the intrepid duo the official seal. His decision was influenced in no small part by the opportunity to advertise it under the slogan *'it's the berries'*, a new popular saying, according to Paolo and Francesca, which had crossed the Atlantic in recent times, supplanting his children's previously endless use of *'the bees' knees'* usually accompanied by uncontrollable giggling.

They need not have worried. Summer sales were a great success. If the café had a trophy to give to its most loyal consumer of *gelato*, Bryn would be its recipient by a mile. Even the fading of the summer and onset of that year's winter didn't diminish Bryn's hunger for a cone and he persuaded Emi to bring some along on match days for the team as the new rugby season began. Most were not as enthusiastic as Bryn about a cold treat on a winter's day and before long Emi found himself bringing hot food and sandwiches for sale to the spectators as well as the teams. It was his plea for help with this new busy sideline that enabled him finally to persuade Ella to come with him to a match. After that she became a regular.

———

As the winter months stretched into the new year of 1926, there was a growing sense of gloom in the area. The local mine was owned by United Anthracite Collieries Ltd and the months of tension between miners and employers nationally had been equally felt in south Wales.

Over a half breakfast one March morning Bryn appeared to be in a dark mood and took little persuasion from his concerned friend to share the causes of his depression. His pride in the local mining community and its history was plain to see as was the pain he felt in witnessing the difficulties it had been facing since the war.

Coal had been in high demand at home through the war. The depletion of seams and reducing production meant that in the post war period other countries were better placed to meet export demands. Prices were driven down by the 1924 Dawes plan which, as part of reparations for the war, led to Germany providing 'free' coal to parts of Europe and in 1925 by the decision of the Chancellor of the Exchequer, Winston Churchill, to re-introduce the gold standard, thus strengthening the value of the pound.

Reduced profits led to mine owners seeking to impose lower wages and longer hours on workers. These were opposed by The Miners Federation. The Prime Minister, Stanley Baldwin, announced a subsidy to maintain miners' wages for nine months and in the meantime a Royal Commission would be set up.

The Commission's report was published in early March. As well as wide ranging reorganisation for the industry, the report also recommended the ending of the subsidy and a thirteen and a half percent reduction in wages.

Now the government had announced acceptance of those recommendations if other parties also agreed. Bryn felt sure there would be resistance, but he did not hold out much hope for success.

In the weeks that followed Bryn's dark mood deepened. Negotiations were failing, strikes were inevitable and at the beginning of May, the Trades Union Congress announced a general strike in support of the miners, albeit limited to transport, railways, iron and steel workers, printers and dockers. The government viewed the strikers as revolutionaries and sought support from the armed forces and volunteer workers.

The general strike ran for nine days. During that time, Gus made the decision to support striking families by providing a free daily meal. That decision could have cost him a fortune, but the strength of feeling in the area was so strong that after a few days some local farmers and producers were supplying what they could by way of ingredients for free, or at a reduced price, to enable Gus to maintain his offer.

On 12 May the TUC indicated an intention to call off the strike if the Commission proposals were implemented and strikers were not punished. The government maintained it had no power to compel employers to take back every striker. Some miners remained on strike, but economic necessity eventually led to the majority returning to work, albeit forced to accept an increase in hours and a decrease in wages. Bryn returned to work feeling nothing had been achieved.

⸺

Emi did his best to maintain spirits within the community during those difficult times. He became a sympathetic ear for many who came to the café and shared their distress over a cup of tea. In truth, however, the strength of his own resolve was under assault from the news he was able to pick up from time to time of his homeland. He continued to read the local press, but Gus was increasingly travelling to London and returning with Italian newspapers.

Over the last eighteen months or so Mussolini had been dismantling the country's constitutional checks against autocracy. Elections, opposition parties and unions were abolished by the Fascist government. Free speech and the freedom to associate as individuals wished were lost. Movements in and out of the country were strictly controlled. Anti-Fascists were brought before tribunals and imprisoned or exiled. Death penalties were imposed and others were killed by Fascist thugs.

Meanwhile, *il Duce* gloried in his authority. Self-sufficiency and, in particular, grain production were promoted. The papers contained photographs of a shirtless Mussolini cutting grain in the fields.

In 1926 there were a number of attempts to assassinate Mussolini. Remarkably, one was made by an Irish woman by the name of Violet Gibson. It was reported that she succeeded only in causing her target a bloody nose.

There were times when Emi felt ashamed that he had abandoned his country at its time of need; that it had been left to acts of bravery from Irish women to challenge Mussolini. What he would give for the chance, at the very least, to bloody the nose of *il crotalo*.

He thought often of Leonardo and wondered how he was. He rarely received letters from him now and Emi had little doubt that his friend was occupied in, or organising, acts of resistance where possible. Emi was concerned for his friend's safety, but could not write for fear of putting Leonardo at even greater risk.

Bryn and Emi had become loyal friends. Emi continued to attend matches even though it was increasingly difficult to sell food at the ground as wage cuts bit ever deeper into the pockets of the community. Most mornings they could be found together chatting in the café for short or longer periods depending on how busy Emi was and how long Bryn had between shifts. Over time, Emi had told Bryn about the life he had left behind in Italy; about his love of Bardi and its people; about the difficult times the population now faced with the rise of Fascism and his worries for his friend, Leonardo.

One Friday morning, late in 1926, Bryn and Emi sat together in the café drinking coffee.

'You know I've been seeing Meghan now for a while Emi?' Bryn began hesitantly.

Emi sensed something major was coming. Bryn and Meghan had an unusual relationship. It had been immediately clear to Emi when he first saw them together that they had known each other for years; there was a volatility to their relationship upon which they both seemed to thrive. Meghan was often seen berating Bryn in public for one reason or another (the subject matter was wide and varied), whilst Bryn seemed constantly to be protesting his innocence calmly and patiently. There were times when Emi wondered why Bryn put up with it, but he was clearly besotted with her. 'She's a marvellous girl Emi,' he would often say. 'She has a fire in her that won't be quenched!'

So now, Emi was convinced that Bryn was either about to confide in him finally that over the years Meghan had attempted to kill him on a number of occasions, or...

'I've asked her to marry me,' Bryn announced.

There was a long pause, which Emi eventually ended when his gesture of encouragement did not produce any further words from his friend. 'Um, are you still waiting for her answer?'

Emi was taken aback when he realised that the lack of a reply was the result of the big man trying to hold back his tears. 'She swore at me,' he said as he began to blub.

Emi was half thinking he would need to find Bryn a stiff drink whilst he consoled him, when Bryn finally continued, 'She told me I was a big idiot. That I had kept her waiting forever. Then she took me in her arms and whispered in my ear "Yes you fool".'

Bryn's blubbing morphed into laughter and the friends stood and embraced. When they sat back down, Bryn asked Emi to be his best man.

NINE

In March 1927 William the Taxi announced that he was organising a trip to Pendine Sands to watch J.G. Parry-Thomas have another go at the land speed record.

Over the last few years, there had been regular attempts to beat the record. In July 1924 there had been a couple of new records set on the road in Arpajon, France; first by Frenchman René Thomas and then, a few days later, by Briton Ernest Eldridge who achieved one hundred and forty five miles per hour. In September 1924 attention had shifted to the seven miles of flat sand at Pendine in Carmarthen Bay where Briton Malcolm Campbell set his first land speed record at one hundred and forty six miles per hour, a speed which he had then bettered in becoming the first man to travel at over one hundred and fifty miles per hour at the same venue in July the following year.

In 1926 another Briton, Henry Segrave, had entered the fray achieving one hundred and fifty two miles per hour in March on Ainsdale Beach in Southport. Then, in April, Welshman J.G. Parry-Thomas had thrown his hat into the ring.

Parry-Thomas had been born in Wrexham. He had studied engineering and in time had become the chief engineer at Leyland Motors, a post which he had then chosen to give up in order to become a full time racing driver and engineer. He co-founded a company based at the Brooklands circuit and went on to win a good number of races. In 1925 he had shifted his focus to the land speed record. From the estate of the racing driver and engineer Count Zborowski, who had died in a crash at the Italian Grand Prix at Monza in 1924, he had purchased the Higham Special, which had been the last of Zborowski's 'Chitty Bang Bang' engineering projects.

The car was powered by a huge twenty seven litre V12 engine that was too powerful for the chassis, so Parry-Thomas set about making modifications which included better aerodynamics. He named the car 'BABS'.

He had run the car at Pendine Sands on 27 and 28 April 1926 and on the second day he had established a new record in excess of one hundred and seventy one miles per hour. His record had stood for ten months, but in February 1927 Malcolm Campbell had returned to Pendine Sands in the first of his 'Blue Birds' and had raised the record to more than one hundred and seventy four miles per hour.

Now, on 3 March, Parry-Thomas and BABS, complete with new body parts, were returning to Pendine to try and take back the record.

William the Taxi had become a bit of an expert in all things related to the land speed record attempts. He had a cousin who lived in Pendine and each time a run was scheduled on the beach, he would travel the short twenty five miles south to meet him. Whilst it was usually possible to see some of what was happening alongside, but set back from, the beach, William and his cousin, Geraint, had taken to climbing to the top of Gilman Point at the western end of the beach which gave a more distant, but clear, unobscured view along the entire stretch of sands looking east. From there they had witnessed each of the Campbell and Parry-Thomas records.

In the end, only Bryn, Emi and Carwyn took up William's invitation. As they travelled in the back of William's car he decided to prepare them for their first meeting with his cousin. 'Geraint used to race motorcycles until he had a bad crash. He's now in a wheelchair.' He paused. 'Thought I'd better tell you that so that it doesn't come as a surprise when you see him.'

When they arrived at Geraint's home, they were invited in and sat around the kitchen table drinking tea. Geraint was a softly spoken man who gave a warm welcome to his cousin and his friends. His wife, Caryl, was welcoming, but it was not difficult to detect a certain tension in the air.

'So, will he do it?' William asked his cousin after introductions had taken place.

'Oh I think so William,' Geraint responded. 'Each time someone turns up at the beach at the moment they seem to be able to nudge the record up a little more. My only worry is whether BABS is really up to it. I think there's only so far she can go and JG doesn't have the financial backing that Campbell does. We'll see.'

'Aye, you're right,' said William. 'It's turning into quite a battle between the kings of speed; they're something special, that's for sure.'

Caryl's groan of disapproval may have been an instinctive response, but it was audible to everyone. There was an awkward silence, which William broke by unwisely asking, 'You alright there Caryl?'

'I'm fine,' Caryl replied in a tone that clearly indicated the opposite. She sighed. 'What is the point though? Why does one man have to be faster than another? Why can't we get from A to B at the pace god intended?...' Her voice tailed off as she re-took control of her emotions in a way she had clearly practised many times before. She left the room.

'Sorry,' Geraint said softly as he followed her.

After Geraint had gone William explained, 'It's been difficult for Caryl since the accident.' He then added, unconvincingly, 'It'll be alright.'

When Geraint returned he was smiling and ready to go. 'Right, we'd better move. You lot have got to get me up that hill!'

They took it in turns to provide the horse power needed to get Geraint to the top of Gilman Point. They weren't the only ones to choose the hill as a vantage point to watch the events below, but there was plenty of room for everyone. On arrival they took in the spectacular view. The beach stretched out before them as far as they could see. Nearest to them people were milling around on the sand below making preparations – BABS was already the centre of attention.

Despite their distance, they could clearly hear the huge engine when it was eventually ignited into life. Emi had been looking forward to this, but the angry roar BABS spat across the sand suddenly made him realise just how powerful the beast was that Parry-Thomas was about to try and tame.

From their viewing point they could see everything below, but when BABS started her run, moving away from them in a straight line, it was not a position from which they could get a real sense of the speed that she quickly acquired in the same way that would have been the case if she had rushed across their line of sight rather than along it. But what they could see was the arrow like direction that BABS took into the distance…until suddenly…the smooth line ahead became violently distorted as BABS skidded off centre and in an instant was tumbling over and over. The power that had propelled her along the beach seemed to take an age to dissipate and when BABS finally came to a halt facing out to sea there was a strange moment of calm. Before she burst into flames.

The audible gasp from those around them led to a silence which still lay heavily upon them as they eventually descended the hill and returned Geraint to Caryl who took him in her arms and persisted throughout their journey home.

That day a new threshold was crossed: John Godfrey Parry-Thomas became the first man to die in an attempt to break the world land speed record.

———

Meghan and Bryn married on the afternoon of 28 June 1927. The time was fixed to enable as many people to attend as possible after the day shift at the mine ended at 2pm. The church was packed with locals; miners and rugby players alike uncomfortably wearing the whitest of shirts with starched collars and ties. The congregation held its breath when Meghan was asked the question, but she said 'I do' in the softest voice anyone had ever heard escape past that fiery tongue.

Everyone attended the Hall after the ceremony. The café laid on cake and refreshments and the local pub supplied barrels of beer. A gramophone sat in one corner playing tunes on a repeating cycle that quickly revealed the limited choice on offer. When it came time for Emi to say a few words, he went for sincerity rather than comedy. He cut the speech short when he saw Bryn starting to well up again.

As the evening wore on, alcohol was flowing freely. Even Carwyn viewed the wedding as a special occasion and was seen to be partaking in a moderate amount of excess. PC Dafydd's face was fixed in a frown of disapproval. Everyone ignored him.

Emi spotted Ella helping Isabella serve more food at the long table set up at the far end of the Hall. When the serving was done, she sat for a while, eyes fixed wistfully on the married couple. He had been certain in his mind for a number of months that he would one day ask Ella to marry him. He hoped she would say 'yes', for he had never met anyone who made him feel so strong, so able to take on the world and cope with anything it had to throw at him. He was secure in his belief that they were meant to be together and to be happy; that it was his destiny to love and protect her for the rest of their lives.

Emi's clarity was dimmed only by his concern for what he could offer Ella. Where would they live? Could he support her on the small income he received from working at the café? Part of him wanted to go over to Ella right now and ask her to marry him; but he resisted the dangers of getting caught up in the intoxicating emotions of a wedding party.

Emi circled over to where Ella was sat. He came up behind her, placed his hands gently on her shoulders and asked her to dance. Soon she was laughing as they did their best to keep in time with the struggling gramophone which became overwhelmed by the volume of voices increasing in direct proportion to the volume of alcohol passing in proximity to their vocal chords. Then Alun Edwards proclaimed with a grin that Emi was 'far too pretty' now his playing days were over. He knocked him gently to the floor and the entire team piled on top of him.

—◦◦◦—

The following morning Emi was up before dawn. He wondered who would be up and about given the sore heads that were bound to follow the excesses of the night before. He imagined that some would be struggling to get to their early shift at the mine on time that morning.

Emi, however, had drunk little and had been determined to be as aware as he could be to witness the long heralded solar eclipse that was due to take place just after dawn. When he got to the café he found Ella sat on the doorstep.

'I wanted to see the eclipse with you,' she explained.

He smiled and sat next to her. They were quiet for a while. The morning sky was cloudy and they feared their patience would be in vain, but then a small gap appeared in the clouds just as the eclipse began. Daylight's energy faded and suddenly the birds fell silent, suspending a repertoire that had gone unnoticed, despite its volume, until it was sharply cut short as if obeying a choirmaster's emphatic hand signal. An eerie lunar shade enveloped the street.

Emi found himself thinking of Leonardo and Luca, wondering if they too were sat watching this spectacle many miles away in Bardi as the moon cast its shadow over Europe. He suddenly felt physically close to them, as if he could turn away from Ella and find them sat on his other side.

'They say there will not be another full eclipse visible here for seventy years,' Emi whispered in the silence. 'Do you think we might make it 'til then and be sitting here together on this step once again?'

Ella took his hand in hers and whispered back, 'I hope so.'

<hr />

Christmas 1927 took place in the midst of a blizzard. After the winds subsided Emi walked to the café in the early hours, shovel in hand, ready to dig away the drifts now settled high against the door and windows.

Although many had sat out the storms at home, Emi could see that mining had not been suspended beyond the usual Christmas Day closure. He wondered what it must be like to spend a shift in the deep black pit and at its end to be dazzled by the crisp white snow that currently covered the surface. Throughout the streets he saw the evidence of miners trudging through the snow: deep black footprints often surrounded by a fine black dust sneezed from the miners' clothes as they shivered their way home.

As he shovelled snow away he saw Ella approaching and noticed that she held a letter tightly in her gloved hand.

'I just saw Isabella and she asked me to give you this,' Ella explained.

He recognised Leonardo's handwriting immediately. He had cleared enough snow from the door to enable them to squeeze inside where Emi quickly made them coffee. As they warmed their hands on the hot cups, he opened the letter and began to read. Ella saw Emi's expectant smile of happiness to be receiving news from his friend become eclipsed by sadness.

'What is it?' she asked.

He handed the document to her. She read the short letter in its neat handwritten Italian script.

Dear Emi

I am sorry to write with sad news. Our dear friend Luca passed away peacefully in his sleep yesterday.

Although we were never certain of his age, in the last few months he began to reveal frailties which suggested perhaps he was older than we thought. He continued to enjoy his walks through the woods, but became tired more rapidly and slept more and more.

I can assure you that he suffered no pain. I have buried him in the woods where he always seemed happiest. I have enclosed a small photograph of Luca which I took in June.

I know his loss will be a great sadness to you, as it is to me, but because of you he lived a good and happy life.

Thank you for entrusting him to me and bringing much needed light to dark days.

Your friend

L'

The small photograph which Emi found in the envelope showed Luca sat facing the camera with his head slanted to one side, as if perplexed by the contraption that Leonardo was pointing at him. The black and white image picked out shades around his face that were lighter than Emi recalled, but the intelligence in his eyes was as sharp as ever.

Emi was silent for a while, staring into the dim light cast by the single bulb illuminating the corner of the café they sat in. He had always missed his loyal friend since leaving Italy, but had felt confident in Luca's happiness with Leonardo. He was suddenly enveloped by a deep sorrow as he imagined a light being extinguished into the darkness that hung over the town of his birth.

Ella stood up and came round to Emi's side of the table. She sat silently next to him and rested her head on his shoulder.

T E N

In 1928 Meghan gave birth to twin boys. She had hoped for at least one girl. Bryn was delighted. Owain and Rhodri were the apples of their father's eye. They were big babies who showed every likelihood of growing into their father's stature. Their birth left Meghan exhausted.

Ella stepped in and helped during Meghan's recovery; she delighted in supporting the care of the twins. Emi visited them soon after the births, as did many others. Isabella brought knitted clothes that were a little delayed due to the need for quite a few extra rows prompted by Ella's report of the twins' dimensions.

Carwyn clumsily joked with an exhausted Meghan that if she were planning any more, 'It would be helpful if you could produce something a little smaller as we need a scrum half.' Bryn let out a laugh which he stifled when he saw the thunderous scowl that descended upon his wife's face, prompting the coach to make an early exit.

The twins were born into difficult times. It was increasingly hard to make ends meet as low wages and unemployment compounded the poverty that locals already endured. Bryn felt lucky at least that he retained employment at the mine. His strength at the coal face enabled him to be productive in ways that some others could not. The guilt he felt when men he knew and respected lost their jobs around him, was tempered only by his determination to feed his family and the exhaustion he felt from the increased production demands placed by the mine on those who remained.

When, in late 1928, his father was laid off from working at the mine, Bryn was overwhelmed with anger and disbelief. His father had worked there for more than twenty years and had never had a day off sick despite a persistent cough that now left him in daily convulsions and which was a cause of increasing anxiety for Bryn's mother. Bryn's instinct was to confront the mine manager, but his father talked him out of it. 'Bryn, you can't put your own job at risk. You have a young family to think about.'

Now Bryn felt responsible for his parents' needs too and did what he could to buy them some extra food each week.

Emi witnessed the hardships faced by the local community and wished there was something more he could do. The café was suffering too through the diminishing trade brought about by the impossible choices and daily struggles that poverty inflicted.

In 1929, as his twenty first birthday approached, Emi struggled with a challenge of his own. He had for some time been planning to ask Ella to marry him when he turned twenty one. On the one hand his concerns about his ability to support Ella were compounded now by his diminishing financial prospects; but on the other, he did not want anything to stand in the way of them being together.

He finally made up his mind. On his birthday, when he and Ella went for a walk, he interrupted their progress on bended knee and asked the question. Ella was wise enough to have seen this coming for months. She smiled down at him and softly told him to get up. Emi looked a little distressed as she wove her arm in his and they walked on slowly.

'You know I'm not twenty one for another two years. If we were to marry now, we'd need my parents' consent,' Ella began.

'Are you saying they would refuse?'

'No, Emi. They adore you and I'm sure they would not hesitate to give their consent.'

He looked confused.

'Emi, I don't want anyone else needing to consent to my marriage. My choice of husband is for me alone. I won't marry before I can give a meaningful consent of my own.' Ella smiled warmly at him. 'You know me well enough Emi.'

Of course, he thought, what was he thinking? He should have predicted Ella's response. Suddenly he felt anxious. 'But will you Ella? Will you say "yes" when I ask you in two years? One word today would be the best possible birthday present.'

'I'll give you three,' Ella replied. '*Si. Oes.* Yes.'

In the autumn of 1929, the stock market in the United States of America crashed. Crop prices fell through the floor and recession became depression across much of the western world. What was already a difficult time in the Welsh mining industry became even worse and mass unemployment followed.

Even Bryn was laid off for several weeks, but was then relieved when he was taken back on with others to keep the mine going.

As time went by the lack of any early signs of recovery led to many in Wales having to make difficult decisions about the future. Eventually, in search of work, people began 'emigrating' to areas of southern England less affected and to further distant destinations. That was a choice which Emi understood, but was not prepared to follow. He had emigrated once already and could not contemplate moving from his adopted home where he felt he now belonged.

Gus did his best to keep the business ticking over, but it proved difficult. He had been careful to keep overheads as low as possible, but Emi started to wonder whether the café could provide enough to keep both he and Alberto in employment.

Gus was spending more and more time in Bristol and it was only when Isabella explained to Emi one morning that Gus's uncle was unwell, that Emi appreciated just how thinly Gus was having to spread himself.

In the summer of 1930 Gus's uncle passed away. It was left to Gus to organise his affairs. His uncle's sole child, a son, had died many years before in an industrial accident of some kind. Gus was gone from home for a couple of weeks and a few days after his return he came to the café early one morning and beckoned Emi to come over and sit with him.

'Emi, there's a rumour around the place that you and Ella plan to marry,' Gus began.

Emi feigned surprise. He knew neither he nor Ella had told anyone, but you did not have to be a genius to see how close they had become.

Gus grinned. 'We are all very happy for you both. You two clearly belong together.' After a pause he asked, 'Have you thought about your future together? Where do you intend to live?'

'I'll admit Zio, I've thought of little else in recent months. You have been very kind to me and I will be forever grateful, but times are difficult and I understand that uncertainties lie ahead for all of us.'

Gus reached out a long arm across the table and briefly held Emi's forearm. 'Emi, you are like a son to me and that will never change. You have shown yourself able to thrive in the face of whatever challenges are thrown at you. Your parents would be very proud of you. As am I.' Gus sat back in his chair. 'Did you know that I tried to persuade your father to come here with me? I wanted us to be partners. I told him that together there was nothing we couldn't achieve.'

Emi looked surprised and shook his head.

'He always gently turned me down,' Gus explained. 'Each time he said *"sono radicato in questa terra"* – I am rooted to this land.' Gus suddenly looked sad. 'For a long time, I suffered the twin guilt of neither feeling as strongly as my brother did about leaving the land of my birth, nor being able to persuade him to join me.'

They sat silently for a few moments. Then Gus said, 'My uncle has left the restaurant in Bristol to me. He was a generous man. He told me there was only one condition to my taking on the restaurant after he had gone: that its name, his name, remains. He told me "I'll die another death if the name changes." Of course, I agreed. It's an exciting challenge, but one that brings tough decisions. In these difficult times I do not see that I can keep both the restaurant and the café running. Isabella and I have talked about it at length and we have decided that we'll need to move to Bristol and focus on the restaurant. We've spoken to Alberto and he wants to work at the restaurant too, so he and his family will move to Bristol with us.'

Gus saw the anxious look on Emi's face and wanted immediately to re-assure him. 'Emi, you too are welcome to join us, but there is another option which I hope you will consider. You have shown yourself very able to run things here. If you wish to stay, I will transfer the business and the building to you. The flat above comes with it and, with Alberto vacating, you and Ella can set up home there when you marry.'

Gus searched for a positive reaction somewhere in his nephew's shocked features. After a moment, Emi seemed to achieve both a smile and a frown simultaneously. 'Zio, I have no money; I don't see how I could afford...'

Gus cut him off. 'It would be a gift. You would pay me nothing. My uncle has been generous to me. It is only right that I am equally generous to you. After all, if your father had joined me, he would have been a co-owner of the café. Think it over. Talk to Ella and let me know.'

Emi thanked his uncle. 'You are very kind Zio.'

Gus hesitated. 'Emi, there is only one condition…'

Emi smiled. 'Don't worry Zio. It will always be *"Agostino's"*…but don't expect me to grow a moustache to match the sign!'

—◈—

When Emi laid out their options to Ella he did not seek to persuade her either way. He explained that they too could start a new life in Bristol if she wished, but Ella was unhesitatingly enthusiastic about the prospect of a life together at the café.

Within a few days Emi and Gus were sat together once again in the café. Before Emi spoke, Gus was careful once more to re-assure Emi that he and Ella were welcome to join them in Bristol.

After a moment's thought, Emi gave his answer. '*Sono radicato in questa terra.*'

—◈—

Things happened quickly after that. Gus had to make the move to Bristol as soon as possible to make sure the restaurant kept trading, even though custom was currently hard to maintain. Within a couple of weeks of their last discussion, Gus, Isabella, their children and Alberto and his family were gone, leaving Emi alone with Ella to run the café.

It felt strange at first, but they both immersed themselves in the task. Trade remained slow, but there was a steady stream of locals calling in, if only to express their support for the new owner rather than make a purchase. Emi and Ella were convinced they could ride out the depression and emerge the other side with a business that could provide for their future.

One morning in November, Emi received documents in the post. He sat with Ella in the café when it was quiet. Together they read through the papers. Gus had spoken to Emi and explained what was required and he had complete faith in his uncle's guidance. Nevertheless, Emi and Ella took their time to read the documents, if only to let it sink in that this was really happening.

Emi ran his finger over the embossed lettering at the head of the accompanying letter announcing the name of the firm of solicitors who had sent it. *Mornacott, Veraby and Reach* asked that the signed documents be returned as soon as possible to their offices in Bristol.

'Are you sure?' Emi asked Ella, pen in hand.

'Completely, Emi.'

ELEVEN

At one minute past midnight on the morning of 18 March 1931, the di Costa household was woken by the sound of knocking on their door. All were woken, that is, apart from Ella, who had remained alert in her bed anticipating that something like this might happen.

She was up immediately and able to re-assure her cursing and half asleep father: 'I think it's someone for me; go back to bed.' Of course, he didn't, instead hovering at the top of the stairs, now joined by his wife, as Ella quickly approached the door in an attempt to silence the increasingly impatient knocking. When she opened the door she saw no-one at first until she realised that Emi was already on his knee.

Emi repeated the question he had mothballed for a couple of years. Ella said 'yes.' Mrs di Costa cried joyfully into her husband's shoulder at the top of the stairs. Emi took Ella in his arms and whispered 'Happy Birthday.'

And so it was that, finally, in the summer of 1931, Ella and Emi got married. It was a simple ceremony followed by a simple gathering at the Hall. Nothing lavish was possible in the current climate, but the couple wanted it no other way in any event. Nevertheless, the entire village attended, glad of something to celebrate in otherwise grim times. Gus, Alberto and their families travelled from Bristol to be there. Bryn readily agreed to be Emi's best man; when he spoke, he went for comedy rather than sincerity. It went down well with the villagers who roared with laughter at Emi's expense.

When it was over, Ella and Emi settled into a life together in and above the café. They were happy. They worked hard. When called upon, Ella still helped out at the school. Emi knew her passion for teaching was undiminished and he encouraged her to find and take any opportunities she could.

In September 1931, the Government abandoned the Gold Standard, bringing some flexibility to the country's economic tool box. This was no panacea, but in the following year there were at least some green shoots of possible recovery.

Confidence slowly began to build and as families hoped for a better future, expansion plans in the Williams household came to fruition in the late summer of 1932. The birth of Alys left Meghan less exhausted than she had been after the birth of the twins and relieved that the boys would have the sound influence of a sister around them as they grew.

Alys' birth ignited Ella and Emi's own plans for a family. They had talked openly about their hopes for a large family, but Emi was, as ever, cautious about their ability to support a growing household until the business was on a stronger footing. Try as he might, he could not shake off his fears for the future. He tried to put his anxieties into words without wanting Ella to feel his enthusiasm for a family was in any way diminished.

Ella listened and reflected, astutely, that Emi's fears remained rooted in what was happening in Italy. He continued to read all he could in the press and she could plainly see how much it upset him. He saw no signs that Fascism was on the wane; on the contrary, its reach was spreading across Europe.

'Emi, I understand your worries, but we cannot know what will happen tomorrow, the following day, or next year,' Ella said to him as they sat together in the flat one Sunday afternoon. 'There will always be a voice of caution in your head. I respect that. I'm afraid we live in a world in which there will always be events around the corner beyond our control. We are strong enough to deal with whatever life has to throw at us – I'm sure of it.'

At the end of September Ella announced, to their mutual delight, that she was pregnant.

In October Ella found Emi reading an article announcing Oswald Mosley's formation of the British Union of Fascists. Were those black tentacles about to find a purchase on these islands? 'It won't find support Emi,' Ella sought to re-assure him. 'Not in this country.'

The turn of the year did nothing to diminish Emi's fears. In January 1933 Adolf Hitler was appointed Chancellor of Germany. The following month the Reichstag was set on fire and, the day after, a decree was made suppressing many liberties in the country. Emi had become depressingly educated in the dark arts of despotism and had little doubt that the Nazis had orchestrated the fire to create a smokescreen under which they sought to justify their subsequent actions.

Ella tried to drag Emi from under the black cloud that seemed currently to follow him around. She enlisted Bryn's help. Emi had not been to many matches that season and Bryn followed Ella's surprising directive one Saturday afternoon in March and took him to the ground for their home fixture.

Over the years, Carwyn's plan and the players' hard work had gradually begun to bear fruit. The team was on an impressive run. After another win that Saturday, Bryn and Emi walked home slowly.

'You know Ella is worried about you Emi,' Bryn said when they had finished some ultimately superficial chat about the match in an attempt to delay what they both knew the primary topic of conversation would be.

'I know Bryn. I keep telling her she needn't worry. I really am very happy; life with Ella is wonderful. I'm a very lucky man.'

'There are times though Emi when you seem to be lost in another world that weighs heavily on your shoulders and I can see, with the baby on the way, why Ella is worrying about you.'

Emi was quiet for a moment and then nodded. 'I'll shake out of it Bryn. This winter is dragging its feet; I'll be a different man come the spring.'

'You will, Emi – you'll be a father. That changes you forever.' After a pause Bryn continued, 'You and I both know that Carwyn can be full of manure at times; his little mantras can get on anyone's nerves. Sometimes, though, he gets it spot on. His latest is "focus on what *you* can control". He says if we each do our job and leave others in the team to do theirs, together we'll be a winning side. It seems to be working for us.'

Emi grinned. 'I get the message.'

Tumble ended that season in 1933 as the first winners of the West Wales Rugby Union Challenge Cup.

At the end of May, Ella gave birth to Maria. Emi's emotions caught him by surprise; he could not hold back tears of joy. Everything changed. The powerful bond he quickly developed with his daughter was plain for all to see. Even Ella looked on sometimes with a sense of wonder. Out of Maria's birth, a wave of optimism began to build that carried Ella and Emi forward on its crest. Emi felt a sense of pure joy and determination that he had never experienced before.

Business at the café began to build back towards the level it had enjoyed before the depression had descended upon the village. Even the provocative headlines of the Rothermere owned press could not dampen Emi's spirits. In January 1934, the Daily Mail published an editorial by Lord Rothermere entitled *'Hurrah for the Blackshirts'*.

A week later the Daily Mirror sought funds from its readership with the headline *'Give the Blackshirts a helping hand'*. There was no sense that such sentiments were shared anywhere in the village and Emi was confident that his family and he were safe among friends.

During that period it sometimes felt as though the village existed in a different time and place, away from the political turmoil of other worlds. The rugby club continued to ride its success, winning the Challenge Cup again in 1934 and 1935, the village and the mine caught up in their celebrations.

In July 1935 Ella gave birth to their second child, a boy. They debated his name at length. They felt instinctively that they should name him after their own fathers who shared the same first name, but a few days after his birth, Emi suggested they name him Leonardo.

'Ella, we are going to have more children and opportunities to give them our parents' names, but I would really like to name him Leonardo. I want to write to tell my friend; to give him news to touch his heart and bring a little joy to his life too.'

Ella needed little persuasion.

Leonardo wrote back in September. *'You both do me a great honour. I pray for the day when we may be together and I might show young Leonardo the biblioteca.'*

TWELVE

In the days that followed receipt of Leonardo's letter, Emi found himself reflecting on fond memories of their time together in the *biblioteca*. In October 1935 Emi had cause to recall their debate about how to categorize the book about the 1896 battle of Adwa. He quickly concluded that Leonardo had been right. In the end, it was all about politics.

Mussolini had been strengthening his forces in Libya and held aspirations of expansion in North Africa. He viewed those countries as being still part of the Roman Empire and Ethiopia, a country that had avoided colonisation, was next within his sights. In October, he invaded.

At the League of Nations the Italian delegation insisted it was not at war, but engaged merely in 'military police measures to establish order'. On 6 October 1935 Mussolini 'avenged' the 1896 defeat by capturing Adwa. The next day the League of Nations declared that Italy was guilty of an act of war, opening the door to economic sanctions which were then imposed.

On 31 October 1935 Emi was in the café. He had been working whilst listening to a news broadcast on the Philco 70 radio which Gus had bought them as a wedding gift. Angry about the pursuit of sanctions at the League of Nations, Italians were holding anti-British demonstrations in Rome.

Suddenly, the door flew open and William the Taxi called out, 'There's been an outburst at the mine.' He did not need to say more. All the men in the café headed immediately for the door and Emi joined them. As many of them as could squeezed into William's car whilst the rest began to run. They all headed for the mine.

Emi was in no doubt about the seriousness of an underground outburst. Bryn had spoken of it many times. He had explained that, under pressure, the coal at the seam can become fine. When there is a build up of methane behind the coal there can be an outburst that spews the gas and fine coal dust into the shaft. Unless there is a quick reaction, there is a risk of asphyxiation from the dust and gas and, even worse, ignition of the gas.

On arrival, those who were miners reported to the team already engaged in rescue work. The rest were ushered behind a perimeter away from any risk of an explosion. Emi looked among those who were present, seeking ways to be useful. He saw Meghan in the background slumped against a wall in tears. Emi's heart sank as he realised Bryn must be down there.

He ran over to Meghan and took her in his arms. She was inconsolable. When she was able to speak, it became clear that she knew little other than Bryn had been leading a team at the seam when the outburst happened and he and twenty two others had not yet come to the surface.

All they could do was hope for news and support those who waited anxiously. Emi set about making hot drinks for the miners who had already surfaced, their faces hidden behind layers of dust of the darkest colour Emi had ever seen, the tone lightened only by the tracks of involuntary tears that had run from their eyes as they had coughed and gasped for air.

Everyone knew that speed was critical. Each passing minute seemed an eternity. Concerns increased when the perimeter for those who were waiting was pushed back even further. Eventually, there was a distant shout from the mine entrance. 'Coming up.' A few minutes later a handful of miners could be seen in the distance walking into the light, some supported by others and some bent double as they coughed and were received into the care of the waiting medical team.

Three more groups emerged over the next twenty minutes or so, each seemingly needing greater support as they struggled to stand. On-lookers were counting off the numbers; it was clear that Bryn was among the four yet to reach the surface.

Ten minutes later Bryn's unmistakable silhouette could be seen. He supported another miner in his arms. The remaining two were carried out on stretchers. Meghan let out a cry of relief, slipped the perimeter and ran towards Bryn.

Bryn was confined to his bed for a week. He struggled to breathe properly for days before his lungs gradually began to clear. In the end, he knew he was fortunate. The two miners who were stretchered out were dead before they reached the surface.

Time convalescing left Bryn unavoidably confronted by the fragility of existence in a form that he was not yet ready to contemplate. Despite Meghan's protestations, he was back at work within a month.

By May 1936 Ethiopia stood defeated. The king of Italy, Victor Emmanuel III, was pronounced Emperor of Ethiopia. The colonial wars were presented at home in Italy as a glorious endeavour, with some propaganda even contending that 'barbarians' were thus being 'civilised'. The truth was revealed ultimately as something very different – brutality, poison gas and death were instead the gifts bestowed by the Italian army who had ultimately been led by Marshal Badoglio. Badoglio was appointed the first Viceroy and Governor General of Ethiopia and later awarded the title of the Duke of Addis Ababa.

The economic sanctions imposed on Italy had led to an even greater national pursuit of self-sufficiency, but the financial cost to the country of its colonial actions was compounded by the additional expense of the decision to send men and equipment to support General Franco when the civil war in Spain broke out. Large tax increases were imposed. Meanwhile it became increasingly clear that Fascist corruption was rife – permits were needed for almost everything, but could only be secured at a price.

Sanctions and Italy's diplomatic isolation were likely contributors to Mussolini's gravitation towards Germany. In October 1936 he and the Nazis formed an alliance.

That was enough to push Emi back into a dark place where he found it difficult to find the oxygen of optimism. Whilst at the end of 1936 and the early months of 1937 the newspapers Emi studied were dominated by news at home of the abdication of Edward VIII and the forthcoming coronation of his successor, he found new depths of despair in reports of the indiscriminate slaughter of innocent Ethiopians over the days that followed an attempt on the life of Viceroy Rodolfo Graziani in Addis Ababa in February.

Such was his state of mind when Francesco was born in the spring of 1937. Emi, of course, loved Francesco with all his heart, but his mind had become dominated by fears about the nature of the world into which he was being born. He worried that a war in one form or another could soon consume Europe and beyond.

In the year that followed, he became obsessed with the need to harvest information and news wherever he could, thinking that if he could have data upon which sound predictions could be made, he would have a head start in securing his family's safety. How on earth he could possibly achieve such a goal, was another matter entirely.

Newspapers and the radio became his close companions. He sometimes felt there was a surreal quality to the information he read and heard; as if it were all just a bad dream. Reports of Europe's slide into the inferno stood awkwardly alongside news of a 'normal' parallel world.

So it was that on the same day in March 1938, Disney's 'Snow White and the Seven Dwarfs' was released into British cinemas and German troops marched into Austria.

Even when Tumble became West Wales Rugby Union league champions in 1938, Emi's anxieties were relieved only for the duration of the post season celebrations and the hangover that followed.

He did his best to avoid reports of the football world cup tournament of that year and was revulsed by pictures of the Italian team dressed in a black kit for their quarter final against the host nation, France, each of them raising their hand in a Fascist salute. He felt no cause for celebration when Italy retained the trophy in the final against Hungary.

News of events in Italy convinced Emi that the nation's descent would be complete. The Fascist press had undertaken a lengthy anti-Semitic campaign and in 1938 new laws were introduced. Jews were excluded from key jobs and banned from schools. They were forced to register with the authorities and restrictions were placed on their liberty.

Pictures of murals proclaiming that *'Mussolini is always right'* made Emi feel physically sick.

In September Emi found himself doubting the sanity of world leaders when he read news of the Munich agreement. Succumbing to German demands regarding the annexation of the Sudetenland left him shocked. 'Walt Disney would have done a better job,' Emi said to Ella as he read his newspaper. 'If they do nothing now, it will embolden him. Peace for our time? I fear our time will be short.'

One Sunday, late in December 1938, Emi was reading a newspaper at home. Sat at the kitchen table, he was subdued and horrified by stories of the looting and burning of Jewish businesses and synagogues in Germany. When Maria pulled at his arm for attention, he reached down and swung her up onto his lap.

'What are you reading?' Maria asked.

'Stories about the world Maria.'

'Read *me* a story,' she pleaded.

Emi searched for something suitable. Maria stopped him as he was turning the pages and said 'Read me that,' as she pointed to a drawing of a large fish.

The report told the story of the unexpected discovery of a coelacanth off the east coast of South Africa. They both needed Ella's help in their attempts to say 'coelacanth' and then quickly decided they would call the fish 'Ceilia' to make it a little easier.

It turned out that everyone thought the species had been extinct for the last sixty six million years, so it was a really important discovery. Emi did his best to help Maria understand how long sixty six million years was. Each attempt involved big numbers that were equally difficult for Maria to imagine and so in the end it was 'a really long time.' She had lots of questions that the story did not assist Emi in answering. 'Where had Ceilia been for all that time?' 'What does she eat?' 'Is she a happy fish?'

When Maria asked, 'What is extinct?' Emi thought that was something he probably could have a go at.

'Sometimes, types of creatures no longer exist. They have no family anymore and so there are none left to carry on.'

'What happened to Ceilia's family?' Maria, quite reasonably, asked.

'I'm afraid I don't know. There can be lots of reasons why some types of creatures disappear. Sometimes there is no food for them. Sometimes the creatures that eat the fish, eat too many of them and none are left. Sometimes things can happen in the world that stop creatures living any longer.'

'Something kills all the fish?' Maria asked, trying to find a singular answer.

'Well,' Emi began, worried now that this was going down a route that he might find it difficult to navigate, 'sometimes that can happen. But look, everyone thought Ceilia was gone forever, but she was strong and waited until one day she was able to prove them all wrong.'

'I like that story,' Maria concluded. 'Hooray for Ceilia!' Maria exclaimed as she clapped her hands together. 'Read me another one.'

———

The following year, all books written by Jewish authors were removed from Italian bookshops. From his many hours of cataloguing the books of the *biblioteca*, Emi knew there were works by Jewish authors among them. In his mind, he pictured those books still standing tall on their shelves in an act of defiance.

Italian Jews had been escaping the country and the papers reported the arrival of refugees into Britain. Emi was aware from his occasional conversations with him, that Gus's trips to London were ever more frequent and the focus of the help being provided had shifted to the refugee community.

By the spring of 1939 all the signs pointed towards war with Germany. Emi was in little doubt that Mussolini would be very likely to take Italy into battle alongside his fellow Fascists. Sure enough, in May, Hitler and Mussolini signed a formal military alliance.

For several months Emi and Bryn had found themselves talking about little other than the prospect of war and its immediate consequences. They wore the features of two troubled men on the days they met in the café over coffee. In May the news of the German-Italian military alliance weighed heavily on their shoulders.

'I don't know what to do,' Emi confessed to his friend. 'I hate the thought of war; of men blindly following orders and killing each other. Such a waste of young souls. Leonardo called the young dead of the last war *"gli uomini traditi"* – "the betrayed men". All that potential to contribute something good to the world laid waste on the battle field.' He paused. 'But he also believed that no one can stand aside and let evil do as it wishes.'

'He was right Emi. It's almost time for everyone to make those hard decisions,' Bryn added.

'I know. This is where I belong Bryn, but there have been times when I regret not having stayed in Italy and resisted the evil that has spread across my homeland at a time much closer to its birth. Could I and others of the same mind have done something much sooner and smothered this demon in its youth before it gathered strength?' Emi's head sank. 'I'm ready to fight this evil Bryn, but I honestly don't know whether I can stand on the battlefield and kill the scared Italian youth in front of me who has been ordered by that snake to go to war.'

Bryn placed his hand on his friend's shoulder. 'I understand Emi. I have been asking myself the same questions. The only way I can answer is that if we go to war it will be to defend the world against an evil that must be stopped. We are not the aggressors here. The Fascists know they can step back from the brink. I hope they will, but if they don't they will find me standing in their way.'

Emi admired his friend's clarity of thought and acknowledged his bravery with a small nod of his head. After a pause he added, 'When the time comes, I'm not even sure if the authorities would let me fight. Will I be seen as one of the enemy? How do I prove whose side I'm on?'

Bryn smiled. 'Tell them to talk to me Emi. I won't leave them in any doubt.'

———

A few days later, Bryn and Emi resumed their conversation. 'I'm thinking of leaving the mine and signing up in the next few weeks,' Bryn told Emi as they sipped their coffee.

Emi's concerned expression could not be hidden.

'If I don't do it now, I'm worried they won't let me,' Bryn explained. 'There are rumours at the colliery that they are going to stop miners from joining the fight Emi. I can't let that happen.'

During the spring, the government had started to make some preparations for potential war. The Military Training

Act had introduced a limited form of conscription, requiring single men aged twenty and twenty one to undertake six months of military training, but there was little doubt that, in the event of war, wider conscription would follow. There had been talk, however, of exemptions for 'reserved occupations' in order not to repeat the mistakes of the last war when essential production for the war effort was affected by wide recruitment of the workforce.

Now there were rumours at the mine that not only would miners be exempted from conscription, but they would actively be prevented from joining up.

'Have you told Meghan?' Emi asked.

Bryn looked down at his coffee. 'I have. She's distraught. I tell her I need to do this for her and the children; for their future. She understands, but…'

Emi reached across to Bryn's great forearm. They sat in silence trying to take in the stark reality of their lives on the cusp of change beyond their control.

When Emi told Ella about his conversation with Bryn, it was clear she already knew. 'Meghan was here this afternoon,' she explained. 'She cried on my shoulder for an hour.'

They sat silently, knowing without any doubt what each was thinking. Ella's eyes could not hide her anxiety. Emi sat next to her and held her close.

Ella broke the silence. 'I know you want to do the right thing Emi. I love you for it. But if you try and sign up, you can't know what they will say. You will be drawing attention to yourself in a way that could lead to things you won't be able to control. My father has warned me about what happened in the last war; about the Germans living in Britain who were detained Emi. If that happened to you, neither this country nor your family would benefit from your protection.'

Emi knew she was right. They decided he would wait to see what happened next. He was angry and frustrated. He surprised himself when later that day, sat at the kitchen table, on seeing a picture of Mussolini in the paper he heard himself hissing. Maria laughed when she heard him and hissed too.

Once he made up his mind, there was no turning back. Bryn left the mine and signed up in July. Everyone tried and failed to replicate his bravery as they said their goodbyes.

At the end of August, posing as the Polish military, Nazi troops undertook border operations, preparing a 'justification' for what happened next.

On 1 September 1939 Hitler invaded Poland. He didn't bother to tell Mussolini before he did so.

THIRTEEN

The scene at the Magnani home on the morning of Sunday 3 September 1939 was no different to that of countless homes throughout the nation. Ella and Emi sat close to their radio with the volume set low so as not to wake the children who had returned to bed for a mid morning nap. For all three to be asleep at 11am was most unusual; their parents were relieved. They could not help but feel that something inside them had guided the three innocents to a dreamworld free from the horror of what was about to be said.

When Chamberlain finished his address, Ella and Emi sat in silence. His words had contained no surprises, but they were shocking none the less.

On the same day that war with Germany was announced, conscription became a reality. Unless within one of the exempted industries (which included mining) or professions, all males between the ages of eighteen and forty one were required to register.

Despite the military pact he signed with Hitler, Mussolini decided to profess neutrality in the war; at least for the time being. Maybe he was annoyed at being left out of Hitler's decision to invade Poland. Emi reflected that Leonardo would say he was just being true to his slippery character and biding his time to see which way the winds of war were going to take the continent.

On 5 September, the United States of America also announced its neutrality.

Emi was not clear whether the requirement to register applied to British nationals only; he assumed it did. In any event he decided to try and persuade Ella that now was the time for him to try and join the British forces. While Mussolini played his games, Emi reasoned, enlistment of Italian nationals might be possible. If he was already fighting the Nazis at a time when Italy later decided ultimately to join forces with Germany, it seemed unlikely he would then face ejection from the British army.

Whilst they were both aware that there were many flaws in his logic, Ella, though terrified of the potential consequences of all the available options, relented.

Emi registered without difficulty, but was then called for interview in Swansea. He was surprised to find that his interviewer held the rank of a Major. He explored Emi's history in detail with a steely efficiency that left his subject feeling he was sat before his inquisitor stark naked. The interview ended abruptly with the announcement that some 'checks' would need to be undertaken and Emi would be hearing from them shortly. On his train journey home, Emi sat wondering whether Pandora had accompanied him to Swansea that day.

Within a week a short letter of rejection arrived. No reason for the negative decision was given. The letter ended, *'You are respectfully required to inform the local police in the event that your address changes.'*

That final sentence left Ella and Emi silently speculating as to its purpose.

'It was important that I tried Ella,' Emi said softly.

Emi constantly gathered whatever information he could from the papers and the radio as the early months of the war developed. Russia occupied a number of eastern Polish territories and subsequently reached an agreement with the Nazis on the country's division between them. Emi was relieved that Bryn had been in touch with Meghan to re-assure her that all was well – he was at a training camp somewhere in Britain at a location he could not reveal. Nevertheless, early British naval losses were deeply troubling. The most shocking occurred on 14 October.

Scapa Flow in the Orkney Islands had established a reputation in the last war as a secure and well defended base for the British Navy, but in the years that followed its defences were neglected such that when war broke out again it was ill-prepared. Thus it proved possible for a German U-boat to enter the anchorage just before midnight on 13 October. It found the battleship HMS Royal Oak at anchor.

Most of the crew were below deck asleep. They were awoken by what they thought was a small internal explosion, but in fact one of a salvo of torpedoes from the U-boat had hit the bow and caused only a muffled explosion. The U-boat reloaded its tubes, fired again and this time tore a huge hole in the battleship. She quickly listed over and then her cordite magazines caught fire. In darkness many of the crew struggled to get out of the depths of the vessel. Within ten minutes she sank.

Less than a third of the crew were pulled from the freezing water. Eight hundred and thirty five lives were lost, many of whom were boys serving their apprenticeships, some as young as fifteen.

U-47 slipped away undetected. The Nazi propaganda machine hailed the achievement and the commander and crew were treated as heroes in Germany. Hitler sent his private plane to bring them to Berlin where he could congratulate them personally. The commander was presented with Germany's highest military award, the Knight's Cross.

Even Churchill acknowledged Kapitanleutnant Günther Prien's 'feat of arms.'

———

In October, the Government had indicated that there would be no repetition of the mass internment that took place in the last war. Numbers were expected to be kept relatively low. That came as a relief to Emi; the expectation was that the focus would be upon German nationals who presented a clear risk to the country's security.

November ended with the news that Russia had invaded Finland and that Ella was pregnant.

They had planned for more children when the time was right; but that condition, patently, had not been met. Emi showed Ella his joy at the news, but never did joy weigh so heavily on their shoulders.

———

In January 1940 food rationing was introduced. Business at the café was reduced almost to a limited number of hot drinks, but it remained a hub for villagers to meet and they were welcomed in whether they ordered anything or not. It became a place to share news of loved ones and what was happening in the war. Newspapers were always kept in a pile in the corner and all were welcome to read them. When news bulletins were broadcast, Emi would turn up the volume on the Philco 70 and all who were present listened in silence.

In April 1940 Herr Hitler, surprisingly and for one night only, entertained the regulars at Agostino's. With a few delicate twists of the dial they had discovered a Nazi propaganda channel targeting, it seemed, the Welsh nation. The broadcast claimed that the Welsh were as different from the English as the Polish were from the Germans. It spoke of the Welsh national spirit that would not be broken in poverty, asking whether it will 'burst forth in revolt?' At that point Dai shouted at the radio in Welsh, 'You're the only one who's revolting Mr Hitler!' Everyone fell about laughing and when the broadcast praised the quality of the Welsh singing voice, they all stopped listening and for an hour sang a series of songs, most of which detailed the comparative lack of virility of Hitler and his generals.

Those newspaper titles which for some years had spouted open support for Hitler and Mosley were embarrassed into a change of direction once war had been declared. They did it with an ease that often left Emi angry. He was desperate for simple news rather than opinion, but the latter continued to find its way into the inside pages. For some, the target became the *'risks'* presented by the alien population of Britain. Stories were printed nurturing rumours that Hitler had a Fifth Column among the alien refugee population. Editorials were written on the subject in nauseating fashion, professing to speak *'on behalf of the people'*.

On the morning of Saturday 27 April, Emi was sat at a corner table in the café about to read a piece on page six of The Daily Mirror for the third time. After the second reading, Emi had forced himself to break away from its content; to take a breather before reading it again, he hoped, with a clearer head. He turned his attention to the three other items on the page.

Two were in the form of advertisements. The first was written by someone who had patently been instructed, no doubt by a team of anxious lawyers, to make it clear that their product would not cure rheumatism, a condition which they confidently asserted was caused *'by poisons that have got into your blood and left a deposit in your joints and muscles'*. Readers were urged *'to sweep out these deposits'* with a daily pinch of their product. Wisely, to cover all possibilities, the piece cautioned *'Don't expect startling results at first (although you may get them) but keep it up, persevere'.* The writer did his best to heed the lawyers' warnings, but he just couldn't contain himself. *'We won't promise you a definite cure'* he insisted, but *'we say this in spite of the hundreds of testimonials we've got from people who tell us they have actually been cured, because we'd rather have you pleasantly surprised with the results you do achieve.'*

The second advertisement was for a make of camera film in the form of a brief instruction on how to be successful when taking pictures, like the one printed in the column of *'Susie and friend'* who were *'somewhere in Somerset'*. Susie's *'friend'* was a piglet who she cuddled in her arms as she looked down at him with obvious pride and affection. The advert was accompanied by a warning:

'Extract from
WAR OFFICE ANNOUNCEMENT:

"Generally there is no ban upon the carriage of cameras in public places by persons other than enemy aliens, who would require a permit for this purpose. It is not forbidden to photograph views or objects except those expressly prohibited items contained in the Orders."'

The third item on the page was a collection of short passages written under the banner *'Cassandra'*. Although Cassandra herself was not pictured, alongside her name was a pair of spectacles through which her eyes alone could be seen. Cassandra reported that *'The Trojan Horse invasion in Norway'* in which a Fifth Column under Quisling had aided the Nazi invasion, *'has given a nasty shock…to His Majesty's Government, who have now suddenly woken up to the fact that there are thousands of British subjects who are Nazis in all but name. They bide their time and work under cover plotting and planning for Der Tag'.*

Cassandra went on to maintain that the leader of The Women's Auxiliary Service, who she described as *'a jack-booted, peak-capped, monocled slip of femininity,'* had in fact recently joined the British Union of Fascists. ***If you look in the Telephone Directory you will find no Iscariots or Quislings. But they are here in our midst, nevertheless.'***

However, Cassandra reserved her most excoriating views for a young employee of the Rhondda Urban Council, who had appeared, unsuccessfully, before a tribunal as a conscientious objector stating that he would willingly serve in the Red Army, but would not take part in a capitalist war. She reported that the lad's father had then stood up and said that his son *'HAD NO OBJECTION TO KILLING AND WAS PREPARED TO KILL ALL THE CAPITALISTS IN THE WORLD'.*

When Emi, finally, returned to the main piece at the head of the page, he read the entire article again. Slowly.

It was headed *'MEMO. TO THE HOME OFFICE'* and was said to be written by John Boswell *'who wants to see some-thing done about a certain Fifth Column.'*

'I know a lot of Italians. I like them all.

We are not, thank heaven, at war with Italy. I hope we never shall be.

But that hope does not appear to be shared, sincerely, by the "too-clever Italian Government." (I thank Herbert Morrison for that brilliant description.)

We have to face facts.

We are at handgrips with Hitler in a fight to a finish.

Hitler has friends.

Outstanding among those is Mussolini, from whom he got his first political inspirations.

Their connection has always been a gangsters' link-up.

When Hitler went to war, Mussolini held back. It was pretty obvious that he was waiting for a corpse to pounce upon.

He was "neutral," he said.

But all the time, through the dirty mouth of his parrot Gayda, he has spewed out a steady stream of poison against the Allies.

In his own time and in his own way, this man lines up against us.

The tommy-gun is greased. The sawn-off shotgun is loaded.

There is a stinking wind from the Mediterranean which bodes no good.

Yet we still tolerate Mussolini's henchmen in this country!

+++

The Government of Italy has thousands of loyal followers here.

Italians by birth.

Fascists by breeding.

And I'm presenting this memorandum in the hope that this fact isn't being overlooked when the various "Fifth Columns" are probed.

England has always been the Job among nations – tolerating everything with a mild smile.

Suffering everything gladly.

People whose native lands failed to afford them the means of a livelihood, thought first of England.

So did the refugees of all the world.

We accepted them, feeling, always, that our democracy was a kind of universal mother.

We gave shelter to a mixed crowd…

Mild men and bitter men; meek and mad men; wise and crazy men; sages and criminals – we have accepted them all.

We took in the poverty-stricken emigrés. That was a good while ago: we could afford to have them, then.

But things have changed.

We live – NOW – in dangerous times.

+++

There are more than twenty thousand Italians in Great Britain.

London alone shelters more than eleven thousand of them.

The London Italian is an indigestible unit of population.

He settles here more or less temporarily, working until he has enough money to buy himself a little land in Calabria, or Campagnia, or Tuscany.

His first object is to start a business; frequently a café.

He often avoids employing British labour.

It is much cheaper to bring a few relations into England from the old home town.

And so the boats unloaded all kinds of brown-eyed Francescas and Marias, beetle-browed Ginos, Titos and Marios.

Settling down quietly in our busy streets, they made small profits and saved with all their might.

And British money went to Italy, to buy Italian farmland for

hard-working Anglo-Italians.

Individually, these people are usually inoffensive, decent and likeable.
BUT...
Mussolini keeps in touch with them constantly.
He has always sent out agents. And the agents, or other zealous Italians, formed Fascist clubs.
So now, every Italian colony in Great Britain and America is a seething cauldron of smoking Italian politics.
Black Fascism. Hot as hell.
Even the peaceful, law-abiding proprietor of the back-street coffee-shop bounces into a fine patriotic frenzy at the sound of Mussolini's name.

+++

The Fascist clubs are very active.
Their function is chiefly social. They enable local Italians to get together for a dance or a game of cards.
But every one of these clubs is in touch with Rome.
Fascist newspapers circulate; the badge of the "Fasces" is worn.
There is much political discussion.
Parents who are members of these clubs have been in the habit of sending their children back to Italy each year for a holiday in a Fascist camp.
In this way the youths learnt the principles of Fascism.
In most cases, they returned to London – British nationals, yet keen and enthusiastic Fascists.
Many of these lads are now soldiers, wearing the khaki of Britain.
Wearing it gallantly, no doubt. In most cases...
But in other cases? What a source of potential danger!

+++

They are, let us say, loyal to Italy, just as we in Italy should remain loyal to Britain.

Italy is Mussolini. And Mussolini seems determined to be our enemy and Hitler's fellow-racketeer.

We are nicely honeycombed with little cells of potential betrayal.

A storm is brewing in the Mediterranean.

And we, in our droning, silly tolerance, are helping it to gather force.

+++

We ought to smoke out our Fascist wasp-nests.

At least we ought to watch them.

Mussolini would never for a moment tolerate twenty thousand such nests of divided loyalty, or worse.

But we always were the mugs of the world…AND WE ARE ALWAYS SORRY AFTERWARDS.[1]

The third reading made Emi feel sick. Was that truly the way the 'British public' saw him? Had he been insulated by the bubble of village life that had made him feel so welcome, whilst the world 'out there' viewed him so differently?

Only then did Emi notice that Dai had been watching him intently from across the café at his usual table. He could see Dai's eyes above his own copy of The Daily Mirror which he held in front of him. Dai closed his paper, got up

---

1 The Daily Mirror – 27 April 1940.
Reproduced with permission of The Daily Mirror/Reach Licensing.

and came to Emi's table where he took Emi's copy from him and walked to the door. Emi could see him outside, through the large window, take a match from his pocket and set light to both papers, ensuring they were nicely ablaze before dropping them to the floor. He smiled at Emi and headed home.

———∞———

Emi felt an urgent need to speak to Gus. When the café was empty later that night, he called him. He too had read the Boswell piece. 'I don't believe there's an Italian in the country who hasn't Emi.'

Emi wanted a view from outside of Tumble. 'Is that what they think of us, Zio, in Bristol, in London?'

'There are certainly some who treat us with suspicion, but not many. They're scared, Emi. They're at war and see danger everywhere. It's understandable. As long as there isn't panic. Fascism is like a disease that creeps across the land. Maybe not before, but now that there is a war they would like to isolate the infected and put them somewhere they can do no harm. If they panic, as they will if the newspapers have their way, they will diagnose only according to a man's place of birth.'

'Is it true, what he says about Fascist clubs in London?' Emi asked.

'I can count on one hand the Italians in this country I have met who will give Mussolini the time of day,' Gus replied. 'Sure there are some social clubs where they share their nostalgia for the Italy of old. There are some Fascist members too, but signing up to membership for many of them is often the product of necessity. It's the only way, for example, they can effectively deal with the embassy or taxes if they own property in Italy.'

Their last words were to promise each other that they would be careful.

On 10 May the Nazis invaded Holland, Belgium and Luxembourg. On the same day, Chamberlain finally lost the confidence of the House of Commons and Churchill was asked to form a government.

Holland surrendered within days and a Fifth Column was partially blamed. Panic and hysteria got their way in Britain and the police were instructed to detain wider categories of 'enemy aliens'.

FOURTEEN

May 1940

'Prime Minister Churchill to Signor Mussolini 16 May 1940

Now that I have taken up my office as Prime Minister and Minister of Defence I look back to our meetings in Rome and feel a desire to speak words of goodwill to you as Chief of the Italian nation across what seems to be a swiftly-widening gulf. Is it too late to stop a river of blood from flowing between the British and Italian peoples? We can no doubt inflict grievous injuries upon one another and maul each other cruelly, and darken the Mediterranean with our strife. If you so decree, it must be so; but I declare that I have never been the enemy of Italian greatness, nor ever at heart the foe of the Italian lawgiver. It is idle to predict the course of the great battles now raging in Europe, but I am sure that whatever may happen on the Continent England will go on to the end, even quite alone, as we have done before, and I believe with some assurance that we shall be aided in increasing measure by the United States, and, indeed, by all the Americas.

I beg you to believe that it is in no spirit of weakness or of fear that I make this solemn appeal, which will remain on record. Down the ages above all other calls comes the cry that the joint heirs of Latin and Christian civilisation must not be ranged against one another in mortal strife. Hearken to it, I beseech you in all honour and respect, before the dread signal is given. It will never be given by us.

Signor Mussolini to Prime Minister Churchill 18 May 1940

I reply to the message which you have sent me in order to tell you that you are certainly aware of grave reasons of an historical and contingent character which have ranged our two countries in opposite camps. Without going back very far in time I remind you of the initiative taken in 1935 by your Government to organise at Geneva sanctions against Italy, engaged in securing for herself a small space in the African sun without causing the slightest injury to your interests and territories or those of others. I remind you also of the real and actual state of servitude in which Italy finds herself in her own sea. If it was to honour your signature that your Government declared war on Germany, you will understand that the same sense of honour and of respect for engagements assumed in the Italian–German Treaty guides Italian policy to-day and to-morrow in the face of any event whatsoever. [2]

---

2 'The Second World War, Vol 2 Their Finest Hour' – Winston S. Churchill. Reproduced with permission of the licensor through PLSclear.

FIFTEEN

When Emi read that Mosley had been detained and interned on 23 May 1940, he tried to persuade himself that the criteria being applied must therefore include some substantial foundation for concern. He was not so naïve, however, beyond that fleeting moment, to believe that would be so in all cases.

In the days that followed, news of the Dunkirk evacuation dominated the airwaves and the printed press. What appeared to be a pending disaster for British and allied forces was hailed as a 'miracle' as sea faring craft of all shapes and sizes answered the call. But the direction of the war, with the surrender of the Belgian army and the imminent fall of France, appeared to be one way only.

At least, that was the conclusion reached finally by Mussolini. He thought he could smell victory for the Nazis and, wanting a share of the spoils, declared war on Britain on 10 June.

In the two weeks that followed, four thousand Italians were arrested in Britain together with three hundred British subjects of Italian descent.

Ella had found ways to cope as best she could in recent weeks by persuading herself that, even if Italy joined the war, no-one would be interested in the tiny Italian population of a small place like Tumble. She was now almost eight months pregnant and when the news of Mussolini's decision broke on 10 June, she could not stop her emotions finding voice, albeit in whispered agonised tones to avoid them being heard by the children. 'No. Please no. No. Not now. Please.'

On Tuesday 11 June, Emi opened the café as usual. 'We have to carry on, Ella,' he insisted, but when he saw the anxiety across her face he added, 'I'll close up early and be home this afternoon.'

In the café he was shocked to hear radio reports of anti-Italian riots on the streets across the country overnight. Some of the worse had been as close as Cardiff, Newport and Swansea. Businesses and shops had suffered smashed windows and looting. Families had barricaded themselves in and in some places the police resorted to baton charges against the mob.

Emi returned to the flat at 3pm. He played with the children who were delighted to have him home at this unusual time. At 3.48pm there was a knock at the door.

Emi opened the door to find Carwyn. He was grim faced and in uniform. Carwyn looked over Emi's shoulder to see Maria at the top of the stairs checking who was at the door before Ella whisked her up and took her into the kitchen.

'Let's take a walk,' Carwyn suggested.

It was sunny and warm as they walked slowly together in no particular direction. 'I've been ordered to take you in Emi,' Carwyn said after a while. 'I got the order this morning and since then I've been trying to speak to HQ in Cardiff just in case it was a mistake. When I finally got hold of them, they just told me to get on with it. I'm sorry Emi; it's madness.'

'You've got your orders Carwyn. I understand,' Emi replied as they continued to walk.

'I'm sure they'll talk to you and you'll be home in no time at all,' Carwyn added hopefully. 'Before you ask, I don't know where they will be taking you. They've set up camps about the country, but no news yet where you'll be. I promise you that any information I get I will pass on to Ella.'

'You know Carwyn, the worst thing is that I am being prevented from supporting and protecting this country and my family for reasons beyond my control. Just because of my place of birth. I am Italian Carwyn. Nothing can change that. Nor would I wish it otherwise. But the man I am is not defined by my nationality. This is my home. You are my friend… It's all falling apart and there's nothing I can do.'

They stopped and faced each other. 'Pack a bag Emi and I'll leave it to you to come to the station when you're ready. No later than 5.30 though please.' They stood silently for a few moments and then embraced.

In the flat the children played whilst Ella and Emi spoke quietly in the kitchen. They each knew how the other felt;

they had unconsciously prepared for this day and only few words were needed.

Emi packed a small bag and they both spoke to the children to explain that he needed to visit uncle Gus for a little while. When he hugged and kissed the children goodbye he wanted to hold them so tightly, but tried not to make it seem that his absence would be anything other than short.

Ella and Emi kissed and held each other tight before opening the door. He assured her that he would be back before long and she assured him they would be fine. She believed, but did not say, that at least he would be somewhere safe, away from the frontline. Emi kissed his hand and held it to Ella's stomach; and then he was gone.

———

At the station Emi was placed in a cell the door to which Carwyn insisted was to be left open. As the night wore on, Emi tried, unsuccessfully, to get some sleep. The night shift at the station took over and Emi was surprised when PC Dafydd greeted him in the uniform of an actual police constable.

It was known throughout the village that PC Dafydd had escaped conscription because of some mysterious medical condition that many speculated about, but none could really identify. Perhaps when the country's need was greatest, he was finally able to persuade the authorities that they should fulfil his dream and accept him into the force.

He looked very smart and stood taller than Emi had previously believed him to be. He held two cups of tea. 'It's quiet out there so I thought you might like one of these,' PC Dafydd said as he sat down on the bunk next to Emi.

Emi congratulated him. 'Thank you,' PC Dafydd replied. 'It's my first week, so I'm still finding my feet a bit.'

'I'm sure you'll do fine,' Emi assured him.

'Look, I'm really sorry about you having to be here you know. It all feels a bit awkward. Can't say I understand it really.'

'Don't worry, no-one does.'

They chatted for a while and drank their tea. Suddenly the bell at the station door rang and PC Dafydd was quickly to his feet. When he returned he had two officers in tow who Emi did not recognise.

'Emi, these officers have come up from Cardiff and are now going to transport you back there,' PC Dafydd explained.

The two officers pushed past their new colleague when they saw that the cell door was open, as though they were afraid Emi would make a run for it. They roughly held Emi's arms and marched him outside to a waiting vehicle. Emi had time only to say to PC Dafydd, 'Tell Ella where I'm going.'

PC Dafydd half raised a hand to the disappearing van in an uncertain farewell.

In Cardiff Emi was taken to Maindy Barracks where he and many others were placed in holding areas. The large room he entered held a group of about thirty men. There was barely time for a few words of shared anxiety between them, before they were packed into a bus before dawn and were transported to the train station. There they joined further men awaiting their onward journey to an uncertain destination.

Eventually they were loaded onto a train that headed north. Emi found himself sat next to a young man, Carlo, who spoke with a strong Welsh accent and who was a British national having been born in Newport to an Italian father who died when Carlo was young. He was dazed, confused and frightened. He did not even speak Italian. Any suggestion that this young man was on the payroll of the Italian Fascist government would be scoffed at on any other day. Emi tried to re-assure him. He told him that in a few days the authorities would see that people like him are no threat and when the panic had died down he'll find himself back home.

Carlo seemed to settle and was soon asleep. Yesterday, Emi would have been sure of the truth of what he had said to Carlo; but today, as the sun came up, he was no longer convinced by his own words.

SIXTEEN

Lancashire – June 1940

Emi had been determined to stay awake through the journey; where were they going? They raced through stations without stopping as he struggled to read the station signs. Eventually he joined the rest of the passengers in drifting, uncontrollably, into sleep.

He awoke with a start when the train came to a halt. The platform sign announced that they were in Bury. Young soldiers stood on the platform in a line the length of the carriages and as the passengers stepped down from the train they were required to form a line two abreast. Once everyone had disembarked, they were set off at a march with the line of soldiers alongside them. Out of the station they headed along the road.

No-one explained how far they were going or what their destination was. Emi had persuaded himself that he and the rest had been 'detained' whilst checks were made. Now, as he marched along the road accompanied by armed soldiers, for the first time he felt like a prisoner. Members of the public stood and looked on, many with unmistakeable features of animosity across their faces. Emi felt humiliated.

After a march of about four miles, their destination became clear. They came to a gate set into a barbed wire fence manned by armed guards. A rusting sign announced that they were entering Warth Mills.

As they passed through the gate, a range of discarded items and debris could be seen scattered in an apparently random fashion across the ground. Ahead was a large building that looked outwardly to be in pretty poor condition. The impression was of a derelict and neglected industrial workplace that had only very recently been occupied by the army. Once inside, that impression was confirmed.

They were directed first into a large room where four officers sat at wooden tables each accompanied by a private. The officers were calling the arriving civilians before them one by one. Emi was shocked by what he saw and heard as he waited his turn.

As each man came forward he was required to hand over his belongings and then remove his clothes. A few questions were asked, but the focus was upon the contents of their bags. Many items were confiscated. Cursory or no justification was given in many cases. Razor blades and pocket knives were seen as potential weapons. Writing and drawing materials were removed as was a typewriter from one man's canvas bag. Wallets were opened. Gold sovereigns, watches, chocolate, cigarettes and even medicines such as insulin were taken. Books were removed in case they were used for coded communications. One man explained that he was a doctor, but could not prevent the confiscation of his stethoscope.

As Emi watched on, he noticed that one officer appeared to be overseeing events as they unfolded. He was sat alone at a separate table and was constantly watching what was being removed. Indeed, there were times when officers appeared to look for an almost imperceptible nod of approval from him as they made choices about what to confiscate. What was clear was that he saw and appeared to approve of many of the confiscated items finding their way immediately and blatantly into the pockets of the soldiers present. The larger more valuable items, however, such as the typewriter, were placed on a table next to him.

This officer, as Emi shortly came to learn, was Major Alfred James Braybrook, who a week or so before had been appointed to take command of operations at the mill.

As Emi waited, he realised that he had brought no items of the type that were now being confiscated. Save one. The contents of the bags being emptied as he watched on revealed much about the decisions taken in the short time the owners were given before detention. He imagined the hurried packing of items precious to a daily life or profession, or the selection by loved ones of small comforts despite the otherwise incapacitating distress that had overtaken them.

When Emi was finally called forward, he handed over his small bag as directed and removed his clothes. The officer seemed surprised by the size of his bag and asked with an obvious smirk, 'Not planning to stay long?' It suddenly hit Emi as he stood there, unclothed, that despite the time Carwyn had given him to pack a bag, neither he nor Ella had thought it necessary to pack for a lengthy absence; as if they both unconsciously imagined that enough for a few days was all that was required, just long enough for Emi to tell the authorities what he thought of Mussolini and the Fascist state.

He realised that he had not even packed a book; Emi, who loved to read. But he had travelled with a pencil and writing paper. He had promised to write to Ella as soon as he could. Given what he had already witnessed, he had practised what he would say when the officer set his writing materials aside before handing his bag back to him.

'My wife is eight months pregnant. I promised I would write to her. Please, I am no risk; please let me keep those.'

The officer snapped, 'In fifteen days you will be given one piece of paper and permitted to write home. Nothing until then. Your serial number is 1658.'

Emi began to protest, but a private took his arm and led him to the next room. There he was given a palias – a straw filled mattress – and a blanket and was told to find somewhere in the mill to make his bed.

The scene that opened up to Emi, as he walked into the heart of the derelict cotton mill, was chaotic. The first sensation that hit him was the smell: a powerful, suffocating mix of old machine oil, bleach used in a random and hurried attempt to give the impression that steps had been taken to sanitise the building and the stagnant canal that ran next to the mill. The space was occupied by the remains of large industrial machinery, stubbornly standing its ground on the greasy cobbled and wooden floors or hanging above them from beams, but both now slowly giving way to rust. The rest of the floor space was taken up by a mixture of rotting cotton, other debris and hundreds of make shift mattresses, some already occupied by the dazed men who had put them there.

Emi wandered amongst the chaos, looking for somewhere to lay his mattress. Eventually he gave up looking for a suitable spot and just dropped his mattress where he stood and sat on it. He tried to take it all in; as did all the new arrivals easily identifiable by their disbelieving expressions. His head sank. He stared for a while at the cobbled floor beneath him.

Suddenly he heard someone call his name. He looked up to find Alberto heading quickly towards him. Emi stood just in time to embrace his friend as he arrived. 'It's good to see a friendly face, Alberto. Are you alright?'

'When did you get here Emi?' Alberto asked.

'I've just arrived. We were brought in by train from Cardiff.' Emi looked around and asked, 'Is Gus with you?'

'I haven't seen him. He was in London when they came for me. I hope he's still out there.'

Alberto looked up and said to Emi, 'You don't want to sleep here. That big glass roof up there is the only source of light here, but the glass is broken or missing in many places – you'll get wet when it rains. Come with me.'

Alberto led him into a dull corner where he had placed his mattress against a wall. He pushed it along to make space for Emi. He pulled one of two pieces of cardboard from under his mattress and gave it to Emi. 'Put that under your mattress to keep out some of the cold and damp.'

They sat and Alberto explained that he had arrived at the mill the day before. Numbers were growing by the hour;

he estimated there were about one thousand five hundred detainees there already and with today's intake it must be getting close to two thousand. Alberto explained that conditions were terrible. 'There's no hot water, just a series of cold water taps for everyone to share. No sewerage system – they've put sixty buckets outside surrounded by canvas. By the end of the day yesterday the smell was terrible. Men have already started removing bits of the canvas to make pillows for their beds.'

As the evening wore on, news of food circulated in equally chaotic fashion. The army made bread, cheese and a mug of tea available from their basic canteen, but it was a free for all with nothing in place to ensure a fair distribution. In the end, some had nothing to eat. Emi and Alberto were lucky to secure a little of each and then lay on their beds. Emi drifted in and out of sleep, disturbed by the cold night (despite the summer weather) and the regular rustle of rats out on night manoeuvres.

The following morning Emi found himself in a long queue for the latrines and a cold wash. In the hour and a half it took him to reach the front of the line, he was struck by the depressed mood of his fellow detainees; there was little conversation between them.

Mid-morning Emi began to explore the site as much as he was allowed. The building was surrounded by two barbed wire fences; the area between the fences was patrolled by soldiers. Many of the soldiers at the mill appeared to be young and inexperienced. They seemed uncertain of their surroundings and wary of their captives about whom they appeared to know little, other than that they were considered an undefined risk. There was a small yard in which exercise could take place.

Emi spoke to as many of his fellow inmates as he could. His experiences at the café as the hub of a community had long since taught him how important it was for people in times of uncertainty to have opportunities to talk.

Over the days that followed, he was deeply affected by the stories of the men he spoke to. There were a few young men, like Carlo, who were British nationals, disbelieving of their own country's treatment of them. He spoke to one Italian father whose British born sons had enlisted in the British army. Only days before his detention he had received news that one of he sons had been rescued from Dunkirk and the other was missing. There were many Italian nationals who had lived in Britain for years, often originating from the mountainous regions of Italy and having travelled to Britain to find work and escape suffocating poverty. The majority of these men were older and struggling more than others to cope with the conditions they found themselves in.

Emi spoke to men of German origin who, similarly, were either British nationals or had lived in Britain for many years. In addition, he learnt that there was a large contingent of German merchant seaman who had been captured by the British navy.

Most shockingly of all, Emi met a handful of German Jews who had been in concentration camps in Germany and had fled to Britain as refugees. They found it hard to put into words what it felt like now to be detained in such conditions in the country to which they had turned for sanctuary.

Emi avoided talk of politics, but a handful of men offered opinions of their captors that made it clear their sympathies lay with the Fascists. But in all save those few cases, it did not require a skilled interrogator to discover that these men were predominantly harmless, innocent and frightened individuals who wished only defeat for the Nazis.

Emi wondered whether the outside world had any idea of the stories and political persuasion of the hundreds of men at the mill. There appeared to be no attempt by those who ran the camp to understand their captives and Emi feared that in the midst of war it would take little for them simply to be forgotten.

Three days after Emi's arrival, conditions were no better. In fact, the continuing additions of more detainees served to make things even worse. The preparation and distribution of food, in particular, remained chaotic and he could see that the older and more vulnerable among the detainees were often left with scraps.

He had decided that he needed to raise his concerns with the authorities. He was loathe to draw attention to himself in case he was considered a trouble maker, but he decided there was nothing to lose. Besides, what was the point of talking to the detainees as widely as he had if he was not prepared to try and achieve some changes given the knowledge of all he was learning?

When the opportunity arose, he approached one of the officers on duty. He asked if he could talk about how food was being distributed to the men and that he was concerned about the welfare of some of them. The look of disdain he received from the officer foretold his response before it formed into words. 'This is not a holiday camp. You'll all make do with what you're given.'

Having received short shrift, Emi wandered out into the yard where he sat against a wall in the sun, troubled and mulling over his next move. After a few minutes he was joined by a man who slid his back down the wall as he sat, letting out a sigh and closing his eyes. 'At least the sun has not forgotten how to provide a warm welcome,' he said.

Emi smiled and held out his hand. 'Here's another.'

Emi guessed the man was in his mid-forties. He wore a moustache above the smile he returned. They introduced themselves and Emi sat quietly next to Cesare Bianchi for a while, eyes closed, both letting the sun's rays envelop them as if replenishing their reserves of resilience.

Cesare then said, 'So, Emiliano, I have seen you talking to the men; listening to them, checking on their welfare. You looked troubled as you sat here so I thought it was time someone checked on you.'

Emi smiled and thanked his new companion. 'That's kind of you. We're all just doing our best to keep going. I just wish I knew what the plan is for us all.'

'Some of the men have heard they intend to hold us here only until we move on to other camps. There's talk of a plan to ship us to the Isle of Man,' Cesare said.

As they talked, they shared their stories. Emi told Cesare about his family, the café and the community in Tumble where he felt most at home. Cesare explained that he had travelled from North Italy to Britain in search of catering work and, through a series of jobs over the years, had worked his way up the culinary ranks. Emi sat in stunned silence when Cesare revealed that at the time of his arrest he was the head chef at the Café Royal in London.

When Emi was able to speak he exclaimed, 'What in god's holy name are they doing arresting the Head Chef at the Café Royal? I'll bet Mr Churchill has eaten your food!'

Cesare laughed. 'People from all walks of life were arrested Emi. Doctors, lawyers, academics. Nor am I the only one here from London restaurants and hotels. There are managers and chefs here from the Ritz, Savoy, Hungaria, Normandie, Café Anglais. Almost the entire brigade from the kitchen at the Piccadilly Hotel is here.'

Emi looked thoughtful. 'Cesare, I'd be very grateful if you could introduce me to all of them.'

———

During the day Major Braybrook occupied a makeshift office in what used to be the shipping department at the mill. It too had fallen into disrepair, but it at least provided a framework which had been reinforced with a second brick wall and a strong door. It was guarded day and night. There were a handful of seats outside the door, where Emi now sat next to a private who had come to collect him from the mill.

Emi had approached a duty officer earlier that day and told him that he had vital information for the commanding officer. When pressed for details, Emi resisted and said that he could only pass it on to Major Braybrook. It seemed that his performance had been sufficiently convincing to prick the Major's interest and now he waited to be called into his office.

When the door opened, the escorting private sprang to his feet and nudged Emi to do the same. The Major's Aide called them in. Once inside Emi stood before a large desk behind which the Major sat, head down, reading a document. Behind and to the right of the Major, Emi noticed a large closed cabinet. On top of the cabinet, Emi could see a few keys belonging to at least two typewriters covered with a cloth too small for the task.

After a few moments, the Major wearily raised his eyes and inspected Emi. 'I am told you have "vital information" for me. Spit it out,' the Major commanded.

'I have important information about the background of a number of the men here, which I believe will be of value to you,' Emi began.

Emi saw that he had caught the Major's attention. The Major found it hard to suppress a little excitement when asking, 'Do I have an informer before me who is going to tell me all about the Fifth Column activities of these treacherous prisoners?'

Wishing to retain the Major's interest for as long as possible, Emi chose not to answer his question for the time being. 'I do not know what is planned for us Major, but I imagine your orders include keeping everyone here alive to avoid any unhelpful comparison that might be made in the press with the poor treatment of men captured by enemy forces.'

Emi thought he may have chosen the wrong tactic as he watched the Major's lips purse and his top button come under a surge of additional pressure. 'You want extra rations for the information you propose to give me – well that depends on the information, doesn't it,' the Major retorted.

'No. I am not asking for anything extra. Major, the rations given to the men are not generous, but the biggest problem is that the kitchen is poorly organised and there is nothing in place to ensure every man is fed a fair share,' Emi explained. He could see that the Major was getting up a head of steam and before he could blow, Emi added 'I'm not saying that it's anyone's fault. It's plain to see that many of the soldiers here are young conscripts who have no experience of feeding so many mouths. That's why I am here. Amongst the men detained here, you have some of the finest chefs and restaurant managers in the country. They are not going to be able to produce fine cuisine with the ingredients on offer, but what they will do is organise and run the kitchen so as to ensure that every man is fed. I have spoken to them. They want to do something rather than sitting around. They're hard workers.'

Emi could see that the Major was disappointed. 'You're wasting my time,' the Major spat.

'Imagine the cost saving Major. The soldiers in the kitchen could be deployed to other duties; the medical attention many men will otherwise soon need because of a lack of nutrition can be avoided. The kitchen facilities are poor, but these men know how to get the best out of them.'

Suddenly the Major's interest appeared to be returning. Money, that was the key; now Emi could see it. Whatever scam the Major had going, money was what Emi needed to focus on. He prepared to add to the list of financial benefits, but the Major raised a hand. 'I will allow a trial period and then take stock. There will be armed guards in the kitchen. Return him to the mill and get a list of the men for kitchen duties.' The Major's attention returned to the document on his desk.

When the green light was given, the new kitchen team swung into action. Cesare invited Emi and Alberto to join them. In no time everything was cleaned and a system was set up with each man having his own clear role. Emi was in awe of the smooth operation that produced its first two thousand meals on day one of the takeover. He could not help thinking that any army would benefit from the military precision that was brought to bear in that kitchen. Emi delighted in seeing skilled professionals at work. The ingredients were basic, but all were treated with care and a meal produced for every man. How Emi wished he had another truffle in his pocket for one of these magicians to create wonders with.

The trial period passed and nothing was said. The Major must have been happy.

—◦◦◦—

Working in the kitchen shortened the days and was a welcome distraction, but Emi had been counting the days since his arrival and on the morning of 27 June he awaited news of writing materials and being able to contact home.

At mid-day he and others were issued with one piece of paper and a pencil. Strict rules were announced. Twenty five lines were permitted and no more. Only English could be written. They were permitted to say they were in Bury, but no further details of the camp could be included. The accompanying envelope must be left open and the letter would be read before sending. Any breach of the rules would result in the letter not being sent.

Emi and a small group of others helped those who struggled to write clearly in English and then he sat and thought carefully about the words for his own letter to Ella. He did not want to waste his opportunity. The paper was glossy and fragile; it took little to damage it. He told her he was safe and well. He said he was in a camp in Bury. He did not yet know where he would be based nor when he would have a chance to argue his case. He sent his love to them all and hoped he would be with them soon… He told her to be strong and to keep safe. All would be well…

Twenty five lines seemed so short.

———

On 30 June, a list of names was read out. It was lengthy. Emi and Alberto were called. So were some of the Italian chefs and managers, including Cesare. Most of the kitchen team, though, were not included. Many of the German merchant seamen were on the list, as were so many of the older Italians.

No-one knew what lay in store for those on the list. Emi became aware of anxiety amongst some who were members of the same family when they discovered that a father or a brother was on the list whilst they were not. There were hurried whispered discussions as some traded places with willing strangers and documents were exchanged to enable family support on whatever path might lie ahead for those who were called.

All those listed were to gather their belongings and be ready to leave. Within two hours they were at the station being loaded once more onto trains. After a further couple of hours, they arrived at Liverpool docks.

There were hundreds of Germans and Italians at the docks from multiple camps. After a long wait they were gradually shepherded into slow moving queues. The speculation up and down the lines was that they were being ferried over to the Isle of Man. They passed through a large shed and eventually emerged onto the dockside. Tied up before them was a huge grey twin funnelled ship. 'Isn't this ship a bit big for a ferry ride across to the Isle of Man?' Emi heard himself ask Alberto.

Alberto shrugged. 'I suppose so. On the other hand, the bigger the ship the more men they can carry across on each journey.'

The line of men ran ahead and up a gangplank onto the ship. As they edged closer Emi could see men entering the vessel and being sent downstairs to the left or upstairs to the right. Alberto suddenly gripped Emi's arm. 'Look – isn't that Gus?'

Emi strained to see where Alberto was pointing. Sure

enough, it looked like him. He was just reaching the top of the gangplank. Emi raised and waved his arm in the hope his uncle might see him, but he did not wave back and seemed not to have spotted him. Gus was directed downstairs to the left. Shortly after, Emi thought he saw Cesare and some of the other restaurant men follow Gus down the stairway.

They finally reached the gangplank and, once at the top, Alberto and Emi were sent up the stairway to the right. They would try and find Gus later. As they passed through the ship they saw mattresses laid out on floors. They looked at each other, both recognising that this ship was not bound for the short hop to the Isle of Man.

What neither of them at that time knew was that the British government had reached an agreement to pass its 'problem' to another country thousands of miles away. Canada had agreed to take and process four thousand civilian detainees and three thousand prisoners of war.

SEVENTEEN

At Sea – July 1940

The SS Arandora was built at Birkenhead by Cammell Laird for the Blue Star Line. At first she operated as a refrigerated cargo ship, taking her maiden voyage on 4 January 1927. In 1929 she underwent an extensive and expensive refit, emerging as a luxury cruise liner and renamed the SS Arandora Star. The fifteen thousand ton liner was promoted as the most luxurious cruise ship at sea.

In 1939 she was requisitioned by the British government and converted into a troop carrier. Her white exterior was painted grey and gun placements were added fore and aft. Many of the expensive fittings were stripped out, but on closer scrutiny it was still possible to identify elements of luxury in the cabins' décor that retained the memories of the ship's former life.

Prior to her arrival in Liverpool, she had been involved in an operation to rescue troops and Polish refugees who had been trapped by the Nazis in southern France. Now her orders were to transport a mixture of German, Austrian and Italian detainees to Canada.

In peacetime the ship carried around three hundred and fifty four first class passengers plus a crew of two hundred. For her journey to Canada she had around one thousand seven hundred people on board. Those consisted of more than one hundred and eighty crewmen, at least two hundred and fifty military guards, over five hundred and sixty Germans and Austrians (of which eighty six were prisoners of war) and over seven hundred Italians.

Most of the Italian detainees found themselves either sent down to deck A in the belly of the ship, or up to cabins on deck D near the top of the ship. It was to such a cabin that Alberto and Emi were directed. As they passed through the door it was shut behind them by a soldier who told them to stay inside and to step out only when directed to do so.

The interior was an awkward mix of opulence and chaos. The walls and ceiling were richly decorated and the elaborate light fittings remained, but crammed into the space available were four bunks with straw mattresses and additional mattresses were spread across the floor, leaving little room to tread. Six men already occupied the cabin. They introduced themselves and speculated nervously about their destination.

By the time they reached the cabin, night was falling. The sounds of men being brought onboard could still be heard for several hours and then there was largely silence. It was difficult to sleep in their anxious state, but it was hot in the confined occupied space and the oppressive atmosphere forced them in and out of light dozes. They became alert when the ship's engines were coaxed into life, but there was no sense of movement for another hour or so.

Finally, at 4am on 1 July the SS Arandora Star slipped her moorings and headed slowly out to sea.

———

By mid-morning small groups of men were permitted to use the toilets, receive a basic breakfast and to exercise for a short time. Outside the upper cabins there were open sections of the deck where they were permitted to walk. They looked out to sea to try and gain some idea as to their direction of travel, but without a sailor among their group it seemed too early in the journey to predict their ultimate course. Emi thought he could hear further groups exercising above them on the promenade deck, but there was no means by which he could see who was there. He was desperate to find Gus. He asked the young guard overseeing their exercise whether he could go up to the deck above, but he was politely told that he was under orders, for now at least, to keep them at this level.

Emi thought he would take advantage of the guard's apparent good nature and asked where the ship was heading. The guard hesitated and then replied, 'We haven't been told whether we can disclose that as yet, so I'd better not say. If that changes, I'll let you know.'

They found themselves quickly back in their cabin until a similar procedure took place in the early evening. They were under the supervision of the same young guard who announced that if they wanted to exercise up on the promenade deck that was now permitted as long as he accompanied them.

They took the stairway up to the open deck where they found other groups of men exercising. Emi quickly scanned their faces in the hope that he would see Gus; but he was not there. He did, however, spot Cesare and managed to catch his eye. As they walked they edged closer together so that they could talk. Cesare had been placed down on deck A. As Emi had spotted him board closely behind Gus, he described his uncle to Cesare and asked if he had seen him. It was primarily Emi's description of Gus's moustache that enabled Cesare to confirm that he thought he had seen him on his deck when they moved through the ship on the way to exercise that morning. Emi asked him to tell Gus that he and Alberto were on deck D and that they would try and find an opportunity to meet. He agreed he would try.

As they walked together they passed a lifeboat station and exchanged a confused glance when they saw that access to the lifeboat was obstructed by a surrounding heavy barbed wire mesh. 'Do they think we will try to escape?' Cesare asked.

'Who knows. Let's hope we don't need to abandon ship,' Emi said half jokingly.

Emi could not sleep that night. Despite tiredness creeping across his body, his mind was racing. Eventually the thoughts and questions spinning through his head became jumbled and confused. They slowly ran out of steam at about 3am and Emi sank into sleep.

On the morning of 2 July 1940, U-47 was heading home to Germany. Captain Günther Prien considered that they had had another successful voyage having sunk eight ships along the way. In doing so they had used thirteen torpedoes, leaving only one remaining in the torpedo bay.

They were about two hundred miles west of the Scottish mainland, with County Donegal in Ireland about one hundred and twenty five miles to the southeast, when they spotted a twin funnelled enemy ship. The sea was calm and although it was cloudy, visibility was good. The ship had no escort and was zig zagging in a standard attempt to avoid enemy tracking. There were no Red Cross markings.

Captain Prien watched through his periscope some two thousand five hundred metres from his target as he gave the order to fire their last torpedo at 0658 and 28 seconds. Ninety seven seconds after the torpedo was fired, he saw a column of water as the target was struck.

—⁂—

When the torpedo hit the after engine room on the starboard side, the explosion wrenched Emi and his companions from their sleep. Electrical power was lost and no central commands could be communicated. They were at first bewildered, but did not panic. Quickly though, they concluded that they should make their way out on deck.

Outside they found soldiers and crew doing their best to direct men to life jackets and to remain calm. Within minutes, however, another guard further along the deck shouted that the order had been given to abandon ship.

With that they were all directed to head up the stairway to the lifeboat stations on the upper decks. Emi could now feel the anxiety that suddenly spread through the men. It did not take a mathematician to recognise that there were only fourteen lifeboats which had been readily visible to the exercising detainees and many more men on the ship than there would be room for. Many of the ageing men were originally from inland mountainous regions of Italy and Emi suspected the majority had never learnt to swim. He anticipated chaos; there had been no lifeboat drills since they had boarded and he knew the assistance of the soldiers would be needed if they were to make it through the barbed wire mesh that restricted the gangways.

Emi grabbed a life jacket and, pushing it into Alberto's hands, he told him to head up to the lifeboats. 'I'm going to find Gus,' he told Alberto. He saw the look of concern on his friend's face, but added, 'Please don't argue with me Alberto, we must act quickly. If Gus and I end up having to jump, we'll need you to spot us from a lifeboat so that you can pick us up. I don't even know if Gus can swim. Go.'

Emi quickly put on a life jacket and took another with him for Gus. He turned and headed in the direction of the stern and the stairway to the lower decks. He soon found his progress slowed by the numbers of men now moving quickly in the opposite direction. He saw a lifeboat come down past the deck as it was lowered from above and its sight seemed to create a greater urgency in those who wanted to reach the safety of one of the remaining boats. It was hard going and it took time for him to inch along the deck. As he finally approached the stairway the ship suddenly began to list. Emi held onto a rail and from above he could see that planks of wood and other items were also now being thrown into the sea. He was shocked to see a man fall or jump from the deck above towards the floating items that had gone before and as Emi took in the scene, dozens of men cascaded in similar fashion from the upper deck into the sea.

Emi suddenly felt the list increase and as it did so he saw the front of the ship begin to lift. It became clear that the ship was rapidly sinking and in minutes the bow would continue to rise and she would sink stern first. Emi hurriedly began an unsteady descent of the stairway. He fell down the last few steps into darkness, slipping uncontrollably down the incline of the passage at the foot. He crashed into an open door which he clung to tightly to halt his slide. There was minimal light through a couple of port holes and it was difficult to see anything much at all, but as he looked down to the end of the passage he could see the movement of water which had already filled the ship's stern to that level.

As his mind raced to try and establish his diminishing options, it was possible to see that the water level was not stable, but was instead advancing up towards him at an alarming pace. Deck A was still a further two decks below his current position. Emi groaned and closed his eyes momentarily; he realised there was nothing more he could do. He prayed that Gus was out. He shouted as loudly as he could – 'Anyone there?' in English and Italian – just in case any survivors were still somewhere in the passage. When no response came, he shouted the same words one more time. Only the reciprocal groan of the ship's frame under stress and the slap of the rising sea level could be heard.

Emi climbed onto the doorframe and took hold of the rail which ran the length of the passage. At first his attempts to use the rail to pull himself back towards the stairs were ineffective as his wet hands simply failed to achieve a strong enough grip. He then felt a bracket connecting the rail to the wall and was able to secure a firm enough hold upon it to pull himself along. He was relieved to find that the brackets were repeated every metre or so and slowly he reached the foot of the stairs. The rise of the ship's bow now meant that the stairs were quickly approaching an angle beyond the vertical. It took almost all of Emi's remaining strength to claw his way back onto the deck.

As Emi planted his feet on the slippery deck, the bow came up a further few degrees and he lost his footing. He held on to the ship's rail and gradually pulled himself up so that he could begin to climb over it. He would have to jump. He tried to find some purchase with one foot on the sloping deck behind him so that he could jump out beyond the ship as she began to slide beneath the waves, but as he pushed, his foot slipped again and he spun in the air as he fell towards the sea. The last thing he recalled was a shooting pain across the centre of his back as he struck something hard in the water.

When Emi awoke he felt wet and cold. He sensed the movement of the sea beneath him and realised that he was in a boat. He was half laying on the floor of what he could now see was a heavily overcrowded lifeboat. The next sensation was a thumping pain that pulsated across his back and which became worse as he tried to move into a more comfortable position. He saw Alberto's face appear above his own from behind. 'Thank god; you're awake,' he heard his relieved friend say.

Emi forced himself into a sitting position to face Alberto. 'Have you seen Gus?' he asked.

Alberto looked away. 'No, Emi.' After a pause he added, 'But we mustn't give up – we've searched the water for survivors, but we don't know who is in the other boats or on the rafts out there.'

Only now did Emi turn his attention to the scene outside the lifeboat. The ship had gone. In her place was a patchwork of debris to some of which clung exhausted survivors. Scattered long wooden planks were embraced by desperate men, creating a load which pushed the saturated wood almost to the tipping point of negative buoyancy. Among the debris Emi counted nine further lifeboats and three life rafts, all over populated. One lifeboat appeared to have a motor and it circled the others calling out words which Emi could not hear. As his eyes became accustomed to the light, he realised with horror that, in many cases, what he thought were pieces of debris were in fact men face down in the water, floating without life.

He turned away unable to process what he was seeing. He looked at Alberto with a silent question on his lips, which Alberto did his best to answer. 'I got to the upper deck. There was chaos. Men became entangled in the wire and when boats were reached most did not know how to launch them. I was lucky. Some of the German merchant seamen knew what to do and I managed to get on board one of the boats they were able to lower. The ship went down quickly.' The words caught in his throat. 'It was a horrible sight Emi. So many men tried, but failed, to get off. I saw some still tangled in the wire as she went down…and then…and then, once she had disappeared from the surface, there was an explosion under the waves – some here say it was the boiler – and then debris and bodies began appearing everywhere as they came to the surface.'

Emi closed his eyes feeling the anguish in his friend's words. Hearing them created images in Emi's mind that left him as horrified as he might have been had he witnessed those scenes for himself.

'We were lucky to find you,' Alberto continued after a while. 'I tried to spot you once we hit the water, but it was difficult. We were heading away from the ship, but before we got too far dozens of men jumped from her deck and we began picking them up.' Alberto looked towards the stern of the lifeboat. Emi followed his gaze and saw a Bryn-shaped man holding the tiller. 'He was lifting men from the water single handed…He's one of the German merchant men; strength of Hercules. Anyway, I heard a bang and saw you laying on debris in the water. You were unconscious and Hercules there pulled you on. It was lucky you hit something hard; I don't think I would have spotted you otherwise.'

A spasm of pain crossed Emi's back as if to emphasise his fortune in circumstances where he could so easily have died. He looked to the stern and briefly caught his rescuer's eye. He nodded his thanks and Hercules nodded an acknowledgment before turning his eyes again to the sea.

Time passed slowly. Emi had no idea how long they had been drifting. He had been scanning the boats and rafts as best he could in the hope he might spot his uncle. He would briefly rest his eyes before starting again and realised that as time wore on some of the survivors in the distance who had been clinging to pieces of debris could no longer be seen. Alarmed by what he saw he encouraged Hercules to try and head in their direction. Weak survivors managed to row slowly against the swell and when they finally got alongside, a number of those Emi had seen holding on had gone. Others who had become very weak were hauled on board even though there was no real room.

Two men who looked as though they had severe head injuries died as the lifeboat drifted. They were respectfully placed over the side and their places immediately taken by two more survivors found clinging to debris with ever weakening resolve.

Suddenly the sounds of the sea were briefly overtaken by the engines of an aircraft. A seaplane flew low overhead and dropped a package. The motorised boat picked it up and then came round to others distributing food, cigarettes and a message that help was on its way. Several hours drifted by before the outline of a ship was spotted on the horizon. As she came closer one of the sailors in the lifeboat recognised the Ensign of the Canadian Navy.

When the Canadian destroyer HMCS St Laurent arrived, her crew threw climbing nets over the side. Somehow, when it was his turn, Emi fought through his back pain to inch slowly up the net with Alberto's help. At the top welcoming hands pulled him onto the crowded deck where he collapsed. He was wrapped in a blanket and found himself with some others in the warmth of the ship's boiler room, drinking hot broth.

The survivors sat mostly in silence during the journey to land, grateful for their lives, horrified and exhausted by their experience. The mechanical noises of the ship dominated the boiler room, but at one point Emi thought he heard one of the Canadian sailors say that the survivors' destination had been Canada before the ship was torpedoed. That same voice said they were now heading to Scotland.

Despite relief at being rescued, Emi found a sudden anger rise within him. The government's plan was to send them thousands of miles away from their families; no opportunity was first being given to prove they were no threat; they were put in harm's way; and now it seemed likely that hundreds were dead. Such a waste of human life, of good men; thrown into the vortex of an ill considered and reckless plan to push a 'problem' beyond Britain's shores.

Emi licked his dry lips and tasted the salty mix of broth and tears of anger, frustration and grief.

Once on land the survivors found themselves in Greenock. On the quay, a long roll call was taken. The names of hundreds of men were met with silence. Emi could not keep count or hear every word in the open conditions, but he did not think he could hear a response when the names of Cesare and many of the restauranteurs were called. Nor could he hear an answer when he heard his uncle's name.

Those with significant injuries were taken to hospital. Eventually the remaining Italians were marched to a school where they continued to arrive in groups. Emi sat watching the door so that he could see if Gus was among later arrivals. He wasn't.

An hour or so later the door opened and a further group of survivors slowly entered. Emi watched closely and right at the back of the line he saw Cesare. Once he had sat and been given some water, Emi headed across to Cesare who embraced him. He had found an opportunity to tell Gus that Emi and Alberto were on board, but he could not look Emi in the eye when asked if he had seen Gus get off the ship.

'I didn't see him,' Cesare admitted. 'I was lucky as I was heading up to the deck when the ship was hit. I don't know if he survived Emi, but I think many were caught by the explosion below deck when the torpedo hit and I saw very few come up from that section of the ship. There may still be hope, but…I'm sorry Emi.'

The following day the survivors were visited by members of Glasgow's Italian community who had heard of their arrival and brought food and clean clothes. The men were given medical checks. Emi was given some pain killers for his back pain.

They were given an opportunity to write home. Emi hesitated over the words he knew he had to write. He told

Ella of his and Alberto's good fortune in surviving. He told her that he had not found Gus but would keep trying. He explained that he was in Scotland, but did not know what would happen next – he hoped now he would remain on land. He added *'I do not know how it is possible for you to write to me or where I will be; I long for news of you and the children. The baby will be due now very soon. I wish I could be there. I feel as though I am letting you down. I'm sorry.'*

Within a few days, officials were at the school taking names and making lists. Some men were preparing to leave, including Cesare. 'Emi, I am leaving today,' he explained. 'They have told us we are being ferried over to the Isle of Man. I hope that's true and we are not heading out to sea again. Maybe I will see you there. If not, stay safe; we must survive this Emi.'

Emi wished him well and they embraced.

Cesare added, 'We have to stay strong for our families… I lost my wife; she died giving birth to our second child. My children can't lose us both. I will pray that you see your family soon. When this madness is over, you and your family will come to my home and I will cook for you my friend.'

Two days later, Emi, Alberto and the remaining Italian men were told to be ready for departure. Unlike Cesare's group, they were not told where they were going and that made Emi suspicious.

A chill ran down Emi's spine when they arrived, once again, at Liverpool docks and saw the ship waiting for them.

EIGHTEEN

The HMT Dunera's single funnel might have given an onlooker the inaccurate initial impression that she did not quite match the size of the SS Arandora Star. In fact, the HMT (Hired Military Transport) Dunera had a capacity as a troop carrier of around one thousand six hundred men. On 10 July 1940 at Liverpool docks, she was now loaded with almost twice that number and ready to sail.

Emi wondered if he was dreaming as he, Alberto and many others who had been aboard the SS Arandora Star only eight days before when she was struck, tried to come to terms with the trepidation they now felt as the Dunera slipped her moorings. Once again, they had no information about their destination and the guards on board appeared to be less amenable to questions and more aggressive than the young soldiers who had been on the Arandora Star. They struggled to comprehend that the authorities were in all probability making another attempt to transport them to Canada.

The ship was clearly overcrowded. Hammocks knocked

against each other, many had to sleep on tables and others, like Alberto and Emi, slept on the floor of larger spaces such as the mess. On the first night, no-one was allowed to step out of the cabin spaces.

The vulnerabilities of the first hours on the Arandora Star felt amplified on this second voyage – no life boat drills, locked in cabins and now guards who barked angrily at anyone who stepped out of line. The survivors of the Arandora Star looked at each other with drawn features and palpable terror as the initial hours ticked by and they strained to hear the slightest sound that might suggest they were under attack. Two days after setting sail they feared that murderous destiny had tracked them down, angry that they had the audacity to survive her last assault.

The loud rasp of scraping metal on metal was heard by many throughout the ship. Those who did froze with fear, waiting for the explosion that would surely follow. The detonation, when it came, was not against the ship. The seamen amongst those on board knew at once that one torpedo had grazed against the hull without detonation and a second had missed and exploded after passing under the ship; but some of those who survived so recently the devastating effects of a torpedo strike, were immediately on their feet and rushing to the nearest door. In desperation they managed to break through one of the door panels only to find a soldier thrusting a bayonet through the door and shouting at them to 'drown like rats.'

Desperation only began to dissipate when it was realised some minutes later that the ship was not at immediate risk. The nerves of some were completely shot; they sat staring into space or hugging their knees to their chest rocking back and forth.

———

Whilst the fear of a U-Boat attack remained a constant amongst many, it was the hellish conditions on board which soon began to take their toll on their physical and emotional health. Hatches remained secured and portholes remained sealed so that daylight and fresh air did not enter. Exercise was limited to twenty minutes on deck once each day where toilets were provided in the form of buckets which overflowed. The deck was quickly awash with urine, faeces and the vomit of those who struggled to find their sea legs. It was impossible to maintain hygiene with what was provided. Twenty men shared a piece of soap and ten shared a towel. Water was rationed. Unsurprisingly, dysentery and skin disease soon took their hold.

There was still no official statement of their destination. The short periods on deck and darkened living spaces gave little opportunity to identify clues, but it was not long before a rumour began to circulate that wherever they were going, it was not in the direction of the North American continent.

The naval crewmen were courteous to their passengers in their limited encounters, but there were persistent stories of military guards mistreating men with impunity, some of which Emi began to witness for himself. It was not unusual for the guards to be verbally abusive when overseeing exercise sessions and on a couple of occasions Emi saw guards strike men with their rifle butts. There was one story circulating that a guard had smashed a bottle on deck and made those exercising walk on the broken glass. There were stories of beatings in locked rooms and, certainly, there were occasions when Emi saw men exercising on deck with facial injuries that could not have been the consequence of an accident. A more recent rumour was that one man who managed to find his way onto the deck at night needing to use the toilet, was stabbed by a guard with a bayonet and was now in the ship's hospital.

Like so many of the men who survived the sinking of the Arandora Star, Emi had lost the few possessions he had with him to the sea. The only clothes he had were the ones he wore and which had been donated to him whilst he was in Greenock. His trousers were already threadbare at the knees, but his jacket was made of a good quality Scottish weave and served him well. It was stiflingly hot below deck, but he removed his jacket only when guards were absent for fear it might be taken. In Scotland he had also been given a pair of thin, fingerless gloves which ended at the fingers' first joint and which he wore most of the time in the no doubt misguided belief that they might offer some protection from the transmission of disease.

There were stories of possessions being pocketed by guards at Liverpool docks when the bags of those who had any belongings were searched before they came on board, but what detainees had left was stowed away out of reach somewhere on the ship such that everyone, in any event, only had access to the clothes they arrived in. Stories also began to circulate that thefts were taking place at night.

After a couple of weeks at sea Emi found himself one night, not unusually, awake after midnight. Sleep for those locked below deck came with difficulty in the heat and when it did it was not always possible to distinguish between those who had succumbed to exhaustion and those who had passed out because of the stifling conditions.

Suddenly he noticed a slowly widening slash of moonlit exterior appear at the door to the mess hall. The outlines of three guards came through and the door was shut behind them. A dull light preceded their movements across the floor as if a torch was being hooded by something dark, retaining all but the weakest of beams.

They paused as they went and the beam appeared to be fixed on the hands and arms of those who slept. Eventually they stopped. One guard held the torch whilst another leaned forward into the beam and placed his hand over the mouth of their sleeping victim. When he woke, the whites of his terrified wide eyes could be seen and the guard held a finger to his lips requiring his silence before using the same hand to unsheathe a bayonet to emphasise the order. The third man then raised the wrist of the prone figure and his wrist watch was loosened and removed.

These well rehearsed actions were repeated by the three guards half a dozen times, sometimes taking a watch, sometimes a ring, before they silently slipped out once again into the moonlight. Emi felt angry, but helpless. His right hand reached to his left and the gold band he wore.

When Emi awoke in the early hours his hand still covered his ring finger. He felt a spasm of pain across his back. At first he had wondered how, during a long voyage, he would tolerate the pains he continued to suffer, but he found quickly that the pain became a companion he almost welcomed. The spasms were like an electrical surge which he convinced himself provided an essential energy and alertness that he would need to survive the journey.

Most of those around him were asleep. Alberto, on Emi's right, stirred and woke. They had a whispered conversation about the events Emi had witnessed overnight. Alberto told him that he knew of one Italian on board who had apparently attached his wedding ring to his penis with a piece of wire, in an attempt to keep it out of sight of the thieving guards. Emi decided against that method of security, but whilst his ring remained hidden under his glove during the day, at night from that time forward he removed it and hid it in a cut he made in the waste band of his trousers.

Later that morning, after some of the men had been outside for exercise, they returned with tragic news. A German internee had been the victim of a theft in which a visa for a South American destination was taken from him and then destroyed. Equally destroyed by the loss, he had jumped overboard to his certain death.

A deep sadness fell across those on board as this news spread. It even seemed to mark the beginning of a change in attitude among some of the guards who, from time to time, appeared to show a greater sympathy for their prisoners.

One of the most abusive among the guards did, however, try to make a sickening joke of the tragedy: 'What some people will do to avoid going to Australia.' His fellow guards did not laugh. Neither did Emi when he overheard those words as he exercised on deck.

NINETEEN

Wales – July 1940

Ella had expressed her gratitude to Carwyn when he had updated her with news that Emi had been taken to Cardiff; she then expressed her frustration when he could not tell her whether he would be staying in Cardiff until things were 'sorted out'. 'If no-one else can, surely the police can find out what the *hell* is going on?'

She felt powerless and for a few days she focused on the café and the children whilst her distress, anxiety and anger were bottled up and mixed into a powerful cocktail. When she could contain her emotions no longer, she sat in the dark after the children were in bed and cried as silently as she could for an hour.

She managed to keep the café open, albeit for shorter hours, where she was assisted by Meghan. Ella's mother looked after the children whilst she was there. Meghan had only occasional news of Bryn, but his letters hinted at dangers to come that he could not share with her. She and

Ella supported each other through the uncertainty and the final few weeks of Ella's pregnancy.

On 2 July Ella received a letter from Emi. It was both short and damaged; it was not difficult to see that he had not been free to write as he wished. At least she knew now that he was safe – in Bury.

Over the next few days the sinking of the SS Arandora Star began to be reported. Ella tried to persuade herself that Emi could not have been on board, given that he had written so recently telling her that he was in a camp. Carwyn apologised that his requests for a list of those who had been on board had not been answered.

The newspaper reports became more detailed. They spoke of there being fifteen hundred internees on board; that many were *'unofficially reported missing'* and that among those unaccounted for were *'a number of well known figures in the London West End hotel and restaurant world...'*

Isabella and Ella had already spoken the day after detentions had taken place. They spoke again when the reports of the sinking broke. Both were equally in the dark, but disbelieving that their husbands could have been on board.

Emi's second letter finally arrived on 12 July. A wave of emotions swept over Ella as she read. He *had* been on the ship. He and Alberto had survived, but Gus...? She took a moment to absorb what she had read. Then she called Alberto's wife. She, too, had received a letter that morning and had already visited Isabella and held her tightly as she broke down on hearing the news.

Ella could hear the pain in Isabella's voice when she

called her next. Her words were of hope that Gus would be found, but she could not hide her distress.

<hr />

There was no news of where Emi was now detained. Ella did not know where she could write to him and she hoped daily for another letter from him. She found herself scanning the newspapers with as much dedication as Emi had always shown, anxious that the only news of his whereabouts might be found in the press. She wanted to know where he was, but feared only bad news would be found in those pages. If she ended the day without reading of further internee deaths, she could continue to believe Emi was safe and well somewhere in the country.

She began to hold on to a hope that he might be released as reports grew of a backlash against the internment policies of the government in light of the great losses on the Arandora Star. Bodies were still washing ashore on the north coast of Ireland and the west coast of Scotland. Early false reporting of fighting amongst the internees as they raced to get to the lifeboats first, was replaced by voices of opposition to the internment policy, including those of the church and notable establishment figures.

Much of the focus was upon the treatment of refugees who had come to Britain for help and who were now being so poorly treated. In a letter to The Times published on 24 July, an American woman living in Britain, Ruth Mulford Robbins, wrote:

'Sir – The need for immediate action to prevent further wholesale internment of refugees from Nazi oppression is so urgent that I beg space to make another appeal. I am an American, drawn from childhood by strongest ties to England, to which my life is now wholly bound, in war as in peace. For Americans, as for other nationalities, the British tradition of personal freedom is an inspiration; as an American whose forefathers fought even the British to maintain this liberty, I feel it my right and duty to make strong protest against the present internment policy which embraces Nazis and anti-Nazis alike.

I am not unaware of the difficulties of discrimination, but they cannot be insurmountable: we dare not let them be, else we lose the battle before it is well joined, for surely fundamental to our fight is the maintenance of the liberty of the individual. Yet in haste and fear we arrest and intern those to whom we have given refuge and whose credentials we are supposed to have examined. This whole policy is degrading Britain in the eyes of the world, and is bringing disillusion and suffering to innocent people and potential friends...'

Without ever meeting her, Ella decided that she and Ruth were as one in their views. It was the only possible conclusion she could reach once she identified in the resolute American's eloquence the words and sentiments that Ella was unable herself to express with such calm authority in the midst of the anger and frustration which she felt. Ella cut her letter from the newspaper and kept it to hand, re-

reading it from time to time when she needed to untangle the knotted emotions that sometimes threatened to bring her to a grinding halt.

On 29 July Ella gave birth to a healthy baby girl. Emi's absence left a void that she did her best to fill with happiness and laughter when Maria, Leonardo and Francesco were brought by their grandmother to meet their new sister.

Emi's absence was hard enough to deal with, but Ella's inability even to know where he was and tell him that his daughter had been born made the reality of their circumstances even more difficult to bear. They had spoken in advance about possible names for their fourth child, but the opportunity to match a name with the miracle that now lay in Ella's arms had been taken from them.

Since it was to her alone now that the duty fell, Ella decided to call their daughter Adelina, after Emi's mother. Her death at his birth had deprived Emi of ever meeting, touching, or hearing the voice of his mother. Ella was determined that he would have the opportunity to do all of those things with this new born Adelina.

Although he was now a fully fledged police constable, locals continued to refer to him by his long standing moniker rather than 'PC Bennett'. PC Dafydd was sometimes unsure whether that was a choice they had made out of affection or scorn, but either way, he knew there was little prospect of it changing unless he took a stand. If he did, Uncle Carwyn warned him, he would look even more of a pompous fool.

He was welcomed in when he called at Ella's flat about a week after Adelina's birth. He gooed and gaed over the baby for a second or two as she lay in her pram, before sitting down and drinking the tea Ella had made for him.

'Have you come with news about Emi?' Ella asked expectantly.

'Ah, no Ella. I'm sorry. I'm afraid we still don't know his whereabouts, but I'm sure he's fine,' PC Dafydd assured her. 'No, I'm afraid I'm here on some official business.'

'Oh. Are you here to arrest me too?' Ella's sardonic laugh was cut short by the serious look on PC Dafydd's face.

'Not to arrest you, no, but I am afraid there has been a breach of the law and I have visited you today so that we can do something about preventing further offences,' PC Dafydd explained in a well practised and formal police manual *now we'll not be having any nonsense* voice.

When Ella asked what she had done wrong, PC Dafydd pointed to the pram in which Adelina had quickly fallen asleep, as if instinctively anticipating a tedious lecture on regulations. Ella looked confused.

'How can I put this?' PC Dafydd began. 'You see, as this is the address of an enemy alien...' He hesitated as he saw Ella's immediate displeasure at his choice of words. 'No disrespect intended...you see, no form of transport is permitted unless it is the subject of a formal permit.'

There was a stony silence, before Ella stood and spoke, clearly unable to hide her disbelief at what she was hearing.

'A pram. A thing for putting babies in. The same pram we've had since 1933 when Maria was born. "A form of transport" you say? *A form of transport.* Do you think I might jump on board and fly down the hill into the village on a bombing run? Do you think the children plan to hide under a blanket and go out on covert overnight missions informing the Nazis about the sweet shop favourites of the average British five year old?' She took a much needed breath. 'You should have been here yesterday; you would have caught Leo red handed converting his soap box cart into a Panzer tank!'

With each word, Ella had been edging closer to where PC Dafydd sat; he was now nervously edging back into his chair. Ella growled with anger. 'Get out! Get out and don't come back unless it's with an apology. Make it as "official" as you like you, you, you…didn't you hear me? *Get out!*'

PC Dafydd began heading for the door, before turning back and ducking under Ella's arm, which extended to a finger pointing firmly at the exit, grabbing the police helmet he had left behind and then leaving as quickly as he could. Ella slammed the door behind him so hard that people in the street looked around as PC Dafydd straightened his jacket and hid his rising embarrassment under a helmet that was two sizes too big for him.

An hour later Carwyn was sat in the chair so recently occupied by his nephew. 'I am sorry Ella. We all know he's not the sharpest. The truth is, the regulations we're being told to follow are not the clearest; frankly, the whole thing's a bit of a mess. Anyway, just to avoid any problems, here's a permit to cover you in case you run into any difficulties.'

He handed Ella a slip of paper which she looked at with disbelief. She began a further indignant protest, but was stopped by Carwyn's raised hand. 'These are strange times, Ella. There is much to be angry about, but let's save our energy for the big battles, eh?' He stood and kissed Ella on the cheek, before heading for the door.

———

Ella was not blind to the wider problems facing the country and she found herself questioning her reaction in the days that followed. She asked herself how Ruth would have responded, but doubted that even she could have remained patient with PC Dafydd.

Young men were losing their lives in the skies above the English Channel as they bravely fought to repel the Luftwaffe in the battle for Britain and her frustration could never outlast the daily news reports of the horrors that the Nazis were inflicting upon the innocent.

Once again, it was in the eloquence of others that Ella found a common purpose. In the same speech, on 20 August 1940, in which Churchill acknowledged that *'Never in the field of human conflict was so much owed by so many to so few'*, he also put the hardships that so many faced into context.

'...Hitler is now sprawled over Europe. Our offensive springs are being slowly compressed, and we must resolutely and methodically prepare ourselves for the campaigns of 1941 and 1942. Two or three years are not a long time, even in our short, precarious lives. They

are nothing in the history of the nation, and when we are doing the finest thing in the world, and have the honour to be the sole champion of the liberties of all Europe, we must not grudge these years of weary as we toil and struggle through them...'

By August 1940 questions were being raised in Parliament about the Government's internment policy. The loss of so may lives on the Arandora Star was viewed by many as a national disgrace; '*a bespattered page*' of the country's history. There were heated debates leading gradually to reforms of the policy.

A White Paper was published which proposed the release of interned Germans and Austrians who were elderly or who could contribute '*work of national importance*' to the country, such as doctors, academics and the like. In late August, a second White Paper applied the same eligibility criteria to Italians.

Ella knew Emi could not meet those criteria, but by October they were revised further to include those who were '*opponents of the Fascist system*'. Finally, Ella thought, Emi will be coming home.

TWENTY

Australia – September 1940

It had taken a while for the news of their destination to sink in. At first Emi felt despair – not content with trying to send them to Canada, they were now to be dispatched to the other side of the world where, no doubt, they could be forgotten. After a few days, his thoughts turned to just getting somewhere, anywhere that could provide him with a chance to argue his case and get back to his family.

The limited improvement in relations with some of the guards had led to opportunities for the internees to access the few portholes that would open – queues were formed and twenty seconds allotted to each man. Those over fifty five and those who were sick were allowed one additional hour each day on deck in the fresh air. Otherwise, little changed and the conditions remained unbearable.

In the third week of August, it having been denied until that point, permission for the internees to shave had finally been given. Whilst it was clearly a step designed to persuade those waiting in Australia that the men had been well treated, Emi struggled to see how the removal of their beards could transform the pale, emaciated figures which remained beneath them. In fact, as he looked at his shaven face in the small mirror provided, he concluded that what was revealed looked a good deal worse.

On 27 August Western Australia had come into sight. A rumour had begun to circulate that all internees would be given their freedom once they had docked. No-one knew how the rumour had started, but Emi saw and heard nothing to suggest there was any substance to it and he had long given up on speculating about what would happen next.

On 3 September, fifty five days after leaving Liverpool, HMT Dunera sailed into Melbourne Bay. Once they had tied up in the harbour, Emi and Alberto found themselves among a large group who were told they were about to disembark. There was disquiet among the remaining men until they were informed that they would be sailing on to Sydney. Those who had survived on the SS Arandora Star were among those who walked unsteadily down the gangway in Melbourne.

Simply stepping onto dry land gave Emi an instant feeling of security that had been absent for the last two months, albeit in his weakened state it took a while to adjust to the absence of the rolling sea beneath him. He took in a deep breath of Australian air, relieved to be outside of the confinement of the ship and away from the constant risk of attack.

The officials waiting on shore could not hide their shock on seeing the ghostly disembarking figures. Shock quickly turned to action as water and food were hurriedly distributed amongst the grateful arrivals. The kindness of those on shore extended to the Australian guards who offered cigarettes as they directed the men onto trains. They headed north to a camp in Tatura, where a series of corrugated iron huts on a hill awaited them.

After a good night's sleep that only the lack of any sensation of movement beneath them occasionally disturbed, the men were given medical checks and treatment was provided where needed. Emi's back was examined with promises of a more thorough medical when he had recovered his strength. In the meantime, a course of painkillers was to be made available to him. It quickly became apparent to those in charge of the camp that, after so long at sea, the men were desperate to be able to write to their families. Writing materials were provided with a warning that it would take many weeks for their letters to arrive in Britain.

Once again, Emi found himself writing to Ella not knowing whether she had any idea where he now was. No rules about what could be said were issued this time around. Emi reflected ruefully that once they were so far away, no-one was really troubled by anything they might write. He explained as fully as he could – he was sorry his letter would take time to reach her, but they were now able to receive replies and he provided the address they had been told could be used for that purpose. He pleaded with Ella to send news.

Stanley Wharton was not a typical Foreign Office recruit. His father was an artist whose best (and worst) work was completed whilst he was heavily under the influence of alcohol. He had somehow managed to persuade Stanley's Swiss mother to marry him during an unproductive sober interlude, when, as an actress, she was on tour in Britain. Stanley's birth within the first year of their marriage marked a return to creativity for his father, but his mother realised, soon after, that she could not live in a home dominated by constant inebriation. When a role was offered to her on stage in Milan, she took it without hesitation, informing her husband only after she and Stanley had already begun their journey.

So began a young life for Stanley touring the great cities of Europe with his mother and his aunt Christina who accompanied them for much of the time, providing the care that Stanley needed when demands on his mother required her to be focused on other things. When he returned to Britain as a young man, although he was not a product of the educational establishments which formed the bedrock for Foreign Office recruitment, his multi-lingual abilities and the ease at which he felt in countries across the near continent, made him an attractive proposition to fill one of the many new roles which became available in the period between the wars.

In London Stanley soon became besotted with the daughter of a minor baronet who he met at a Foreign Office function, but when their stormy relationship of some eighteen months ended with her telling him he had become 'boring', his first instinct was to find a new challenge as far away as possible. When he became aware of a languages post to be filled in the intelligence section at the High Commission in Australia, what was an unattractive career option for most others, proved to be just what he was looking for.

At the end of October 1940, his department head directed Stanley to be part of a team being sent to interview internees who had arrived in Australia from Britain. The team had access to a report written by an Australian medical army officer by the name of Alan Frost, who had been appalled by the condition in which he had found the nearly two thousand internees who had disembarked in Sydney from HMT Dunera on 6 September and were then sent on to Hay in southwestern New South Wales.

The team's task was to take statements from the internees about their treatment during the voyage for the purposes of an on-going investigation. Stanley was truly shocked by the testimonies he took. He quickly discovered that, in addition to having been so poorly treated at sea, very few of these men represented any kind of threat to Britain.

In early December, after a month in Hay, Stanley was directed to head to Tatura, north of Melbourne, where a further small team had begun a similar task with a group of about five hundred internees who had also been on the Dunera. There he found men who were mostly on the road to recovery from their experiences and keen to tell their stories.

When Emi shook the outstretched hand of the official from the High Commission who introduced himself as Stanley Wharton, he was instinctively cautious and not yet certain whether he was ready to be as candid with him as Mr Wharton, in his introduction, was now urging him to be. Emi's trust in British authority was in a fragile state and he felt justified in expecting this man sat in front of him to say something beyond platitudes. 'You say you are taking our statements, but what are you going to do with them?' Emi asked.

'Let me be frank. I'm a long way from the top of the food chain when it comes to decisions about this stuff,' Stanley replied, 'but I don't believe we would be putting this amount of time and effort into this inquiry in wartime, unless someone at the top had decided that it was important to find the truth.'

Emi nodded silently. He told Stanley his story; from his detention in Wales to his disembarkation in Australia. 'Thank you,' Stanley said at the end. 'I'm sure it means little to you, coming from a junior official like me, but I'm truly sorry you and others have been treated in this way.'

'Given none of this was ever your decision, you don't need to apologise,' Emi responded, warming to the human being before him, if not the institution behind him. 'But thank you.' He went on, 'I'm glad our treatment on the Dunera is being taken seriously, but you will understand that none of this deals with why we are here in the first place. I and most others here are not Fascists. We are thousands of miles from our families and after being so long at sea it was our hope that once on land, even so far away, we would at last be given the chance to show who we are and make our way home. Yet here we are three months after arriving and nothing seems to change.'

'I was sent here for the purpose of the investigation only, I'm afraid,' Stanley replied. He paused and looked at the man before him whose life and those of his family had been turned upside down so suddenly. 'I can't promise anything, but I will try at least to get some answers for you.'

As Emi rose to his feet, Stanley saw the grimace of pain that shot across his face. 'You're in pain?' Stanley asked, 'Has the doctor seen you?'

'When I got here. I'm told another doctor will examine me soon, but I've got pain killers. I'll manage. I just want to go home.'

———

Just before Christmas, a long letter arrived from Ella. Emi read it ten times before putting it safely back in its envelope. It was the first word he had heard from home in six months. He read Ella's disbelief that he was on the other side of the world. He read how much they missed him, how long it had seemed since they saw him last, about the children…about the birth of Adelina. About Isabella…and her grief. He read the question he could not answer: '…*when will you be home?*'

The following day Stanley found Emi. 'I hoped to give you some kind of news before Christmas. All I am told at present is that everyone's case will be reviewed in the coming months. There is a suggestion that some of you may be shipped back to Britain for a review there, but nothing certain. I'll keep asking. Attitudes have been changing in Britain about the internment policy. There are, shall we say, 'regrets' at the highest level. Maybe there will be something more certain in the new year. I'm sorry.'

'Thank you for trying,' Emi said. After a pause he asked, 'Will you be with your family for Christmas?'

'No, I'm on my own down here.'

Emi looked at the newspaper folded beneath Stanley's arm and decided to say 'I like to read the news. If you have finished reading that, would you be willing…?'

Stanley handed the paper to him before Emi finished his question. 'Here. Merry Christmas.'

TWENTY ONE

North Africa – December 1940

The stakes in North Africa were high. Control of the Suez Canal and access to the oil reserves of the Middle East, were both vital. It did not take long following Italy's declaration of war on 10 June 1940, for battle to be joined. On the 14th the British Army crossed into the Italian colony of Libya from Egypt and captured Fort Capuzzo. The Italians took time to gather their forces in Libya and then on 13 September 1940, they slowly advanced into Egypt. After just fifty miles, they set up a number of fortified camps at Sīdī Barrānī. They did not then move any further forward for weeks.

In October Mussolini invaded Greece from Albania. The campaign was a disaster and needed the intervention of the Germans the following year. Their intervention would also be needed in North Africa.

Allied forces in North and East Africa were vastly outnumbered by the Italians. British forces were under the command of General Wavell who had been appointed in

July 1939 when steps were taken to enhance protection of the Suez Canal. The large Italian forces in Libya were under the command of Marshal Graziani and faced an allied force in Egypt of only thirty six thousand, made up of British, Indian and New Zealand troops.

Rather than sitting and waiting, General Wavell had already used some of his armoured troops to maintain regular raids over the Libyan border. By December 1940, a mobile armoured force under General O'Connor had been assembled. They were still vastly outnumbered, but they now included three additional armoured regiments that had been sent to Africa in a hurry.

When Bryn concluded his training in 1939, there was considerable debate among his superiors about how best to utilise their sizeable new asset. There was talk of shoe-horning him into a tank, but a major priority at the time was the preparation of vast numbers of new conscripts. Thus it was that, having impressed decision makers with his calm determination and physical abilities, he found himself under the command of a hardened sergeant-major assisting in the physical training of raw recruits.

Bryn continued to impress. He was quickly promoted to corporal and in late July 1940 he volunteered for training for a special force that was being put together for active operations in North Africa. At the end of November Bryn arrived in Egypt, where he joined his new unit, the Long Range Desert Group.

The LRDG was first formed in North Africa in July 1940 by Major Ralph Bagnold. Before the war he had become an expert on desert navigation and communication and the operation of vehicles in extreme conditions. His idea was to put together a lightly armed unit for long range reconnaissance and intelligence gathering behind the Italian lines in Libya. The initial intake was made up of New Zealanders, but they were soon joined by Southern Rhodesian, British and other nationalities.

After a short period of further desert training and acclimatisation, Bryn was quickly sent out on operations. The roles of the patrols were varied. There were occasions when they were required to execute combat operations, but their expertise in desert navigation meant they were also ordered to guide other units and agents across difficult terrain.

Perhaps their most important role was the clandestine monitoring of traffic behind enemy lines, passing intelligence gained on to Army HQ. They used light vehicles, stripped of all but the essentials to extend their range and navigated with the aid of a sun compass devised by Major Bagnold himself, which, unlike the standard issue compass, was unaffected by magnetism and could be used accurately whilst driving.

It was during a monitoring mission that Bryn engaged with enemy troops for the first time. He and his sergeant were well camouflaged, observing a road from a distance of about three hundred and fifty yards. They were in separate positions about one hundred yards apart. Their vehicle was also camouflaged, two miles behind them, between two rocky outcrops.

They spotted an Italian patrol of two soldiers in a single vehicle pull off the road and circle into a position that placed them behind the prone British soldiers. They were so close that any movement from Bryn to turn and face them would have been obvious. All he could do was wait and listen to every sound which might indicate an approach to his or his sergeant's positions.

For a while, the two Italian soldiers appeared to be chatting outside their vehicle, but after about ten minutes Bryn heard the sounds of approaching footsteps followed by liquid hitting the floor as one of the Italians relieved himself. Bryn held his breath. His rifle lay next to him. In view of the need for stealth, he and others often had an unholstered side arm at hand as well to avoid the obvious sound and movement that drawing the weapon would require. Bryn's side arm of choice was a captured standard issue Italian Beretta M1934; its reliable feeding and extraction cycle left him confident it would not jam if needed.

After a pause, Bryn cursed silently to himself when he heard hesitation, followed by slow but deliberate steps towards his position and the cocking of a weapon. At the least, the enemy soldier had spotted something suspicious. Bryn carefully gripped his pistol and tried to judge the point at which he could no longer wait. When the footsteps paused and then became even more cautious, he rolled onto his back, raised his pistol and fired in one movement.

His bullet hit the chest of the young Italian whose shock only caused the shortest of pauses before he adjusted the aim of the rifle now pointed at Bryn. Before he could shoot, Bryn fired twice more and the Italian fell.

Bryn looked immediately for the whereabouts of the second Italian. He saw him laying next to the enemy vehicle already dead. Bryn's second and third shots had masked the sound of the single rifle shot that his sergeant had got away as the second Italian's attention focused on the gun fire at his comrade's position.

Having broken cover, they quickly hid the two bodies as best they could and took the Italian vehicle, together with their own, back to base under the cover of night.

Only in the early, adrenalin dissipated hours of the morning did the true horror of those events hit Bryn. He vomited quietly outside his tent. He could not shake the image of the young man whose life he had taken, his dead, staring eyes still showing disbelief that the moment of his death had arrived so soon. Bryn knew he was in a war; that he was trained to kill; that if he did not kill, he or others would be dead. But he also knew nothing could ever prepare him for the act of taking a life. He was sickened by the thought of what he had done that day, but also by the knowledge that he would unhesitatingly kill again.

—⊸∞⊸—

On 7 December 1940 General O'Connor's armoured forces had been mobilised. By 9 December they had already taken three Italian garrisons. On 10 December, the cluster of Italian camps at Sīdī Barrānī were flanked on both sides by Allied forces, attacked and taken.

The 7th Armoured Division pushed west to isolate Tobruk until the Australians could join British forces and mount an assault. On 21 January 1941 Tobruk was attacked. It fell the following day. At Beda Fomm on 7 February the Italian 10th Army collapsed. With those gains, the way was open for the Allied forces to push along the coast all the way to Tripoli, but instead, a large part of the North African forces was redeployed to fight the Nazis in Greece.

The opportunity was lost.

The Nazis recognised that they would have to send help to the beleaguered Italian forces. In February, Lieutenant-General Erwin Rommel was appointed commander of the new mechanised Afrika Korps. In the second week of February he arrived in Tripoli with only some elements of the two divisions that would take several months to become fully assembled, but he quickly set about an offensive with what he had. Encouraged by his progress, he pressed on and by the second week of April British forces had largely been pushed back into Egypt. The only exception was the garrison held by the 9th Australian Division at Tobruk who repelled the Nazi attempts to take the fortress. Two attempts to relieve Tobruk failed. A disappointed Churchill removed General Wavell to India.

Having succeeded so quickly in dealing with the Italian forces in North Africa, the British were now to find the Afrika Korps under Rommel a much more difficult opponent. The campaign would swing one way and then the other for months to come.

TWENTY TWO

Australia – June 1941

By the end of February 1941 Stanley had completed his interviews at Tatura. When at the camp, he had tracked down Emi from time to time and, whenever he could, he would hand over a newspaper or two. They were mostly Australian papers, but on those occasions when he had to visit the Melbourne office he was also able to pick up some British papers that tended to arrive many weeks after their publication date. He had belatedly discovered that the guards at Tatura were under instructions to cut out any articles relating to the war before passing newspapers to their Italian guests. Stanley had not personally received a similar directive and thought it ridiculous that these men so far from home and their families, should be deprived of news of events in the outside world. What possible malevolent use could they make of such information? Once it came to his knowledge, he therefore decided to feign ignorance of the usual practice.

In so far as their respective positions allowed, Emi and Stanley became, what in normal times an observer would unhesitatingly call, friends.

Once the interviews had finished, they did not think they would see each other again. They had said their farewells. But in June, Emi was surprised to see Stanley's smiling face at the door of his hut. 'I'm back,' Stanley announced. 'More work to do.'

They stepped outside where Stanley explained that as he and his team had already built up a knowledge of the men on site, they had been asked to gather information from them that would assist in the formal review of individual cases, whether those took place in Australia or back in Britain. 'I wanted to say "hello",' Stanley added, 'but you'll appreciate that while I do this, I'll have to play the part of a stuffy, stand-offish official. So not too many visits I'm afraid. Look, I've got you some interesting reading.' Stanley handed Emi a number of newspapers and added, 'I know you'll read the lot, but I've marked a few pieces I think you'll want to look at.'

'It's good to see you,' Emi said as Stanley headed off to start work.

Although there were reports Stanley clearly wanted him to see, Emi decided to read the papers chronologically. It was the only way he could fill in and make sense of the gaps in his knowledge of what was happening in the world over the last six months. He laid them out in order – a mix of publications from Britain and Australia.

He read reports of a broadcast Winston Churchill made on 9 February effectively telling the United States of America to provide support: *'Give us the tools and we will finish the job.'* He read about the arrival of the Afrika Korps in North Africa and the ebb and flow of the brutal battles that were taking place on that continent. And he read about Swansea.

From 19 February Swansea had faced three nights of intensive bombing. During fourteen hours of attacks almost nine hundred high explosive bombs had been dropped, killing an estimated two hundred and thirty people and injuring many more. The town centre was almost completely obliterated.

A chill ran through Emi's spine and briefly numbed the back pain he had continued to suffer. The thought of that attack only twenty miles away from his family in Tumble left him cold. Ella had made no mention of this in her letters. No doubt, Emi reflected, she did not want him to worry. But with this news, the endlessly simmering frustration he felt at being so far from home, boiled over into anger. He stood and went outside where he found himself punching the iron wall of his hut until his hands hurt. He had to find a way back to his family.

When later that day Emi resumed his reading, he soon reached the first of the articles that Stanley had marked.

'ALLEGED THEFTS FROM INTERNED ALIENS' was the headline to a short article in The Times dated February which stated that Major Alfred James Braybrook, forty six, of the Corps of Military Police had appeared on

remand at a court in Bromley where four new charges were put to him. He had already been accused of *'stealing 100 gold sovereigns, two typewriters, jewellery, 1040 razor blades and other articles belonging to enemy aliens who had been interned at camps of which he was commandant.'* The new charges concerned *'the alleged fraudulent conversion of £365 entrusted to him for the purpose of financing a canteen at an internment camp of which he was commandant'* and *'the theft of a number of sixpenny novels from interned persons.'* He pleaded *'Not Guilty'* and was committed for trial at the Central Criminal Court.

The second marked article was dated May. It reported the Nazis now accepting that U-47 had been sunk by British depth charges in the Atlantic in March. It stated that there had been reluctance on the part of the Nazis to admit the loss of their great hero, Captain Günther Prien, who had been responsible for the sinking of HMS Royal Oak, SS Arandora Star and many other ships, but now they had finally done so.

Until that point Emi had held no knowledge of the identity of the captain who had ordered the firing of the torpedo that had killed so many men on the Arandora Star. In his mind it had always been Hitler and his Nazi thugs who had given the order and the British government who had placed them, unprotected, in the cross hairs. Nothing would change that.

The final marked article was also dated May 1941. It reported the court martial at Chelsea Barracks, London of a number of soldiers who had served on HMT Dunera. Among the punishments were *'severe reprimands'*, *'demotions'* and, in one case, *'a twelve month prison sentence'*.

When Emi next saw Stanley, he thanked him and his team for their work.

―⊶―

Although they spoke less often during his new enquiries, Stanley still managed to maintain a steady supply of newspapers for Emi, who was always catching up with events that had occurred some weeks before.

He read about the liberation of Ethiopia from Italian forces and the return in May of Emperor Haile Selassie to Addis Ababa.

He read about the Nazi invasion of Russia that had begun in June. Emi was at a loss to understand the madness that influenced Nazi decision making. In the previous two years the Nazis and Russia had agreed various strategic pacts and yet now the Nazis launched a huge operation against Russia over an eighteen hundred mile front. The indigenous populations of the east were facing deportation and genocide. Nazi evil appeared to know no bounds. Surely now, Emi hoped, Hitler was spreading his forces across the globe too thinly. Surely now Allied forces could defeat him if they worked together?

He read about Major Braybrook's trial at the Central Criminal Court. He was found guilty and sentenced to eighteen months' imprisonment.

―⊶―

Stanley thought it best to ask one of his colleagues to meet with Emi when they got to him on their list. The junior clerk who interviewed Emi was clearly focussed on his checklist and, unlike Stanley, showed little interest in the human being sat in front of him.

Date and place of birth were confirmed. Circumstances of arriving in Britain, activities and employment whilst in Britain were all dealt with in perfunctory fashion. 'Are you now, or have you ever been, a member of a Fascist organisation?' asked the clerk.

'Never,' Emi replied.

'Do you hold, or have you ever held, sympathy for any Fascist state or organisation?'

'Never.'

The clerk put his pen down and sat back looking at Emi. 'What do you think of *il Duce*?' he asked, whilst maintaining his observation of Emi's reaction.

Emi was amused by the young official now staring at him. His cocky attempt to be clever and improvise away from his script was clearly the product of his deluded belief that he was blessed with the most cunning of interrogatory skills.

'A friend of mine always called him a "rattle snake". Let me be clear, I think Fascism is evil. The people of Italy deserve better.'

Emi needed something to keep him busy when he had nothing to read. He wrote regularly now to Ella and counted the days each time as he awaited her reply. The option of physical activity wasn't always an easy one for him. He had seen another doctor who had thoroughly examined his back with much tutting as he explored each vertebra in his spine. But after much shaking of his head, sucking air through his teeth and making notes, the doctor just prescribed more pain killers. Emi wasn't sure if it was his back or his endless frustration at waiting for his review, but there were increasing numbers of occasions when he felt a tension in his body that led to spasms of pain.

The guards remained largely friendly towards the inmates and the pursuit of hobbies and education were both encouraged. In time Emi discovered two young internees, Giuseppe and Giovanni – 'Peppe and Gio' – who, like Carlo who Emi had met on the train to Bury, had been born in Britain to an Italian parent and, for one reason or another, had grown up with next to no knowledge of the Italian language. At their request, Emi quickly set up a daily language class. Each morning at 0930 Peppe, Gio and Emi could be seen walking the grounds of the camp as the teacher administered his quickfire vocabulary test, pointing sharply at surrounding objects.

For a while, Emi and Alberto spent time thinking of new ice cream flavours they could create and that might be popular after the war was over, but without the means to experiment and taste their increasingly outlandish ideas, they soon lost their enthusiasm.

One morning Stanley came by with a newspaper for Emi and told him that he anticipated groups of internees would shortly be moving to Melbourne before sailing back to Britain. The plan was that they would attend tribunals on the Isle of Man. 'I have no say who goes on the lists, Emi,' Stanley explained. 'I just do the interviews and send a copy of the replies to the set questions up the line. Anyway, I just wanted you to know. If you're not on the list, don't worry. Anyone who doesn't travel will have a tribunal here. If that happens and you're released, you can travel home a free man.'

Emi wasn't sure which he would prefer. He wanted to get back to Britain, but if he ended up languishing for months on the Isle of Man waiting for a tribunal, it might be better to get that done with sooner in Australia. When he saw men leaving for Melbourne over the coming months, he changed his mind. He just wanted to close the vast distance to his family.

In October 1941 Alberto's name was called and he prepared to leave. When the time came, they embraced and encouraged each other to believe they would soon be free to go home to their families.

Tribunals at the camp began in November. Only a few occurred at first. No lists or schedules were published; they just had to wait. As far as Emi could gather, most of the tribunals that did take place were successful for the internees concerned.

By the end of the month no date had yet been set for Emi's tribunal. On 7 December Japan attacked Pearl Harbour. War had come to the Pacific.

—✦—

Priorities and resources all shifted in the direction of the Japanese threat. Stanley was required in Melbourne and those who sat on the tribunals were given duties elsewhere.

On 15 February 1942, the British garrison in Singapore surrendered to the Japanese after a week of fighting. Ninety thousand British, Australian and Indian troops were based there. Four days later, on 19 February, the Japanese carrier force that had attacked Pearl Harbour launched an assault on Darwin in north Australia. Ships in the harbour were hit, two airfields attacked and the town was devastated.

Emi could see there was little point in asking about his tribunal in those early months of 1942. When writing to Ella he tried to stay positive. In the spring she wrote with the good news that Alberto had been released after a tribunal hearing on the Isle of Man. That gave them both an injection of optimism.

The tribunals resumed in May. Still Emi was not called. Then, one morning in July, Emi was informed that his case would be heard that afternoon. He had played over in his mind what he intended to say a hundred times during the waiting months and now, suddenly, it had all become a little jumbled. He sat quietly throughout the morning, re-marshalling his thoughts.

The tribunal was making use of the camp's administration building. He joined a handful of other men sat outside the large room at the back of the building that afternoon as they waited for their names to be called. All of the other men present entered and exited the room as Emi continued to wait. He watched closely as they came out. Most could not hide the look of relief on their faces. It was infectious and Emi smiled back at them as they stepped out the door into freedom.

Emi was the last to be called as the afternoon was drawing to a close. He was shown by a guard into a room that was largely bare save for a long table at which three seated men faced him and a chair in the middle of the room to which Emi was directed.

The chairman of the tribunal was studying a document on the table in front of him and after Emi was seated it took him some further minutes to finish his reading and raise his eyes to Emi. He wore reading glasses over which he now peered and a moustache that Emi could not avoid judging as a poor attempt to attain the high standard set by Gus.

'Ah, Mr Magnani,' the chairman began. After a pause he added, 'This shouldn't take long,' a comment seemingly directed more to his fellow tribunal members than to Emi.

It was a comment that gave Emi a slight surge of confidence that his case was a straight forward one.

'Now, as you will know,' the chairman continued, 'we have been asked to consider whether there are men here who have been interned by the British government, who should now be released. Essentially, we are looking to establish whether you are in fact an opponent of the Fascist system, rather than a supporter of it, such that you do not present a real risk to the security of the country in this time of war.' He paused and studied Emi. 'Do you understand?'

'I do sir,' Emi replied.

'Good. Now I have here a note of your responses when interviewed. It states that you replied when asked that you have never been a member of any Fascist organisation and nor do you hold any sympathy for any such organisation or state. Is that correct?'

'That is correct.'

'I see,' the chairman concluded. 'Your answers are very clear.' He turned a couple of pages in the document on the table before him. 'Therein, Mr Magnani, lies the problem. We have very clear evidence, you see, that you joined a Fascist organisation in Italy some years ago.' He paused only long enough to witness the look of shock and disbelief on Emi's face, before adding 'So you will readily understand, Mr Magnani, that the combination of membership of such an organisation and lying to deny that fact, must lead to the inevitable conclusion that you do indeed represent a risk to the security of the country.'

Emi was stunned. When finally he was able to form audible words, he said 'It's not true. It must be a mistake. I have never been a Fascist.'

The now impatient chairman interjected, 'The *evidence*, Mr Magnani, clearly says otherwise. Take him away.'

Emi tried to plead his case further as the guard took his arm and led him from the room, but the men on the tribunal were already standing and heading for a side door. Emi was escorted back to his hut where, despite spasms of pain, he sat outside slumped with his back to the wall and his head in his hands. What the hell just happened?

On a still August morning Emi sat dejectedly outside his hut. There were fewer and fewer internees at the camp and the growing emptiness, whilst a joyful sign for those to be released, only added to his low mood.

It had become apparent that some men, when given their freedom, had elected not to take passage home when it was offered, unable to contemplate another dangerous two month voyage across the seas. Instead, they had decided to take up offers of wartime work in Australia. Whatever the dangers, Emi longed for the opportunity to take one of those empty berths.

He had just completed a letter to Ella. He had decided against telling her what had happened at the tribunal for the time being. Given the short notice, she had not been aware of the hearing and he did not want to alarm her any further. First, he felt he needed to find a solution to the difficulties he now faced. He had thought about trying to contact Stanley and asking for his help, but he wasn't sure how he would react to the tribunal decision and, in any event, he did not know how to reach him.

As he sat pondering his predicament he heard approaching footsteps. When he looked up he saw Stanley stood a few yards away wearing a cautious expression. 'How are you?' Stanley asked.

'I'll admit I'm struggling Stanley. Can I assume from the look on your face you've heard about the tribunal?' Emi asked.

'I have. I thought about coming sooner, but I've been stuck in Melbourne and…' He paused. 'Look, how can I put this? I felt I had to understand the evidence they're holding for myself. I want to believe you, but in my position…well, I have to be sure.'

'I understand.'

'It seems they have lists,' Stanley explained. 'Lists of people who have been members of Fascist organisations. God knows how they get these things, but in war I suppose access to this kind of intelligence comes from all sorts of sources. Anyway, your name is on a list. There is little information beyond that, save it says you joined in 1923. I suppose you would have been pretty young then. I'm an employee of the Foreign Office Emi. Unless you are able to show this information is wrong, I have to treat you as a Fascist sympathiser. Do you understand?'

Emi had stopped listening once he heard the year in which he was alleged to have signed up. His mind was rapidly thumbing through the records of his life until he got to 1923. He would have been fifteen,...that year he...and then it hit him.

'Stanley, listen to me. In 1923 I saw an application in my name to join the *Avanguardia Giovanile Fascista*.'

Stanley looked confused.

Emi went on to describe his discussion with Signor Pavani at his kitchen table when he had been looking for work. 'I don't know what happened to that form Stanley, but it's the only thing I can think of. Maybe it just got mixed up with the other workers' applications and was sent unsigned to the local party administrator. Maybe...maybe Signor Pavani forged my signature? Maybe he thought it was the only way to give me the work I so desperately needed at that time and he was scared of repercussions for him and his family if he employed someone who was not a party member? I don't know Stanley, but I promise you, I have never applied to join the Fascist party. The very thought of it makes me sick.'

Stanley looked pensive. 'Maybe you're right Emi. But I don't see how we can prove it. Were it not for the war I suppose we could just ask Signor Pavani, but... I'll do what I can, but I'm not sure there's much chance of changing their decision.'

TWENTY THREE

North Africa – September 1942

In November 1941, the Allied forces in North Africa had launched an assault on the Nazis as Rommel was pursuing an offensive of his own against Tobruk. A number of confused tank battles had followed. Rommel had moved towards the Egyptian border, intending to try and cut off the Allied forces, but, having out run his fuel supplies, his attack stalled and the Allied forces were able to push him back and then relieve Tobruk on 7 December.

Rommel had begun a further offensive in January 1942. Allied forces had failed to replace their earlier losses and they were overstretched as a result. This enabled Rommel to make some gains. He was slowed by heavily mined Allied defences, but eventually he broke through, captured Tobruk and pushed Allied forces back into Egypt.

The Western Desert Force had been re-designated as the Eighth Army and in August 1942 it had come under the command of Lieutenant-General Bernard

Montgomery. He quickly set about restoring equipment, supplies and morale.

———◦———

Bryn had become an experienced operative in the LRDG and in 1941 he had been promoted to sergeant. He was unlikely ever to forget the circumstances in which he received news of that promotion; his commanding officer congratulated him as he sat dazed and bemused by news from Meghan that Emi was in Australia!

Throughout 1941 and the first half of 1942, Bryn had been regularly involved in activities behind enemy lines. They had continued road watch missions, each lasting for up to ten days at a time and had conducted raids on enemy rear positions. There had also been a mission to pick up men from what later in 1942 became known as the Special Air Service, who had parachuted behind enemy lines and who they had then taken on to a raid on Nazi airfields.

The airfield raids had destroyed many aircraft and other vehicles. The tactic initially used had been to enter a base stealthily, place Lewes bombs on the aircraft and vehicles and then leave before they exploded. The Lewes bombs were light and combined explosion and fire as a result of the plastic explosive and diesel oil content. However, during a second raid at Sirte, the attackers had done away with stealth once on the airfield. They had driven their trucks between the rows of parked aircraft destroying them with grenades and machine gun fire. Units had supplemented their army issued weapons with surplus Royal Air Force aircraft guns with a high rate of fire. They mounted pairs of Vickers K and .303 Browning Mark II machine guns on the vehicles, a pair of the latter having a combined rate of fire of two thousand four hundred rounds per minute. The success of the mission had led to this method becoming the standard form of attack.

With the Eighth Army now holding the line at El Alamein, plans were put in place in September 1942 to attack German and Italian supply lines and major ports. British Commandos were to attack Tobruk by land and sea, the SAS were to attack Benghazi and the Sudan Defence Force were to capture the Jalo oasis. The LRDG were to guide the attacking forces to their targets and also provide a force to attack Barce, northeast of Benghazi in Operation Caravan.

The town of Barce was an Italian administrative centre with a large airfield on the northeastern side. The airfield was to be the primary target. Further diversionary targets were to be the barracks to the southwest and the railway station in the south. The force put together for Operation Caravan consisted of seventeen vehicles and forty seven men, including Bryn's unit.

They set out from their base in Egypt in early September on an outward journey of one thousand one hundred and fifty five miles. They travelled in a mixture of Chevrolet trucks and Jeeps. Since about June 1941, the LRDG had added a Heavy Section equipped with trucks used to provide logistical support by transporting supplies to bases and establishing hidden replenishment sites at pre-arranged locations. On this long journey, they were accompanied by two of the Heavy Section trucks for their initial refuelling needs and then they were to rendezvous with two more trucks later along their route.

The force was under the command of Major Easonsmith. The two patrols making up the force were led by Captain Timpson and Captain Wilder. They were also accompanied by Major Vladimir (known as 'Popski') Peniakoff and two Senussi tribesmen. Peniakoff had founded and was the commanding officer of No.1 Demolition Squadron, known as 'Popski's Private Army'. He had been born in Belgium to affluent Russian émigré parents. He studied in Belgium until the German invasion in 1914, when his father took him to Britain where he then studied at Cambridge. In the 1920's he emigrated to Egypt and worked there as an engineer, learning desert skills. He could speak multiple languages. In October 1940 he was commissioned in the British Army and joined the Libyan Arab Force, also known as the Sanusi Army.

On this mission, the two Senussi tribesmen were to operate as spies, arrangements having been made for them to gather information about enemy positions from contacts near Barce and then to report back shortly before the planned raid.

After only three days Captain Timpson's Jeep overturned at the top of a sand dune. The resultant injuries led to his and the driver's evacuation. After eleven days, on 13 September, they set up camp fifteen miles south of Barce under the cover of a line of trees where they prepared their equipment for the raid. What they did not know at that stage, was that they had been spotted during their journey and alerts had been passed on, resulting in enemy preparations against their anticipated attack.

At dusk on 13 September the force set off towards the

target area, cutting telephone wires as they progressed. Near the outskirts of Barce a sentry challenged them at a police checkpoint. He was successfully disarmed, but another Italian was shot and the LRDG attacked the checkpoint buildings with hand grenades. At the checkpoint one of the gun mounted trucks collided into the back of a wireless truck when the column stopped suddenly. The gun mounted truck's radiator was destroyed. After being stripped, the truck was abandoned.

One of the wireless trucks separated from the rest of the column to monitor radio messages and act as a rendezvous point after the attack. When the column joined the main road they drove forward with their headlights on, pretending to be an enemy convoy. At the top of an escarpment they came under fire from two small Italian armoured vehicles that were quickly dealt with by heavy LRDG machine gun fire as they raced by.

By midnight they were at the crossroads outside Barce and the two patrols separated to carry out their respective missions. Bryn's patrol headed to the airfield, skirting the eastern side of the town. Close to the airfield entrance the patrol was challenged by sentries who were shot down. The gates were shut, but unlocked and they simply pushed them open and drove onto the airfield.

The attack developed swiftly. Bryn was on one of the machine gun positions and he fired at the first target on the airfield, a truck and trailer carrying aviation fuel which ignited. The fireball it created illuminated a significant section of the airfield making it easier for the patrol to navigate the area.

Although an attack had been anticipated, the Italians had been convinced it could not be mounted from the main road and so they had positioned their forces in the south, anticipating an attack on foot. As the patrol attacked the administration building and barracks with grenades, there was consequently little opposition.

They then targeted a hangar and other buildings, some motorised transport and a fuel dump before heading onto the airfield where they drove in single file shooting at parked bomber aircraft. They also had time bombs in the last vehicle of the column and as they passed any aircraft not already on fire, two men jumped out, ran to each plane and placed a bomb on top of the wing above the fuel tanks, which then exploded after a short delay.

The drivers were experts at manoeuvring at high speeds, making them difficult to hit, but it was also clear that the anti-aircraft guns defending the airfield could not lower the angle of their aim sufficiently to hit targets on the ground. None of the men were hit and no vehicles were put out of action during the hour spent on the airfield.

After the raids, the two patrols met at the rendezvous point before striking a course home. The force as a whole had lost ten men, three trucks and a Jeep. Before dawn the following morning they came under fire, suffering injuries and further vehicle damage. Those vehicles that had to be abandoned were destroyed with explosives. During the day they also came under attack from the air until they were, once again, protected by the arrival of dusk.

Vehicle losses were now high and those still running could not transport all the men, a number of whom were wounded. Ten men set out to walk to a rendezvous point where a vehicle had been left. The force doctor took the last remaining truck and a Jeep with the wounded, reaching a landing ground near the Kalansho Sand Sea. The RAF then evacuated the wounded to Kufra.

Bryn had joined another party of fourteen men who set out walking, whilst their rations and water were carried on the last remaining Jeep. After about eighty miles, on 17 September, they met an LRDG patrol.

Searches of the area were undertaken and eight of the first walking party were found. The two missing men had fallen behind and, after walking one hundred and fifty miles on foot, they reached an Arab camp. However, needing urgent medical attention, the decision was made to hand them over to the Italians and they became prisoners of war.

By October 1942 Montgomery had acquired an advantage in numbers of men and equipment and was ready to launch an offensive. During the night of 24 October the Allies began a six hundred gun barrage, under which the Eighth Army attacked enemy positions. Ten days later, after fierce fighting, the German line was breached. Benghazi and Tobruk were quickly retaken.

The United States of America, having entered the war after the attack on Pearl Harbour, had started providing direct military assistance in North Africa in May 1942. In November 1942, under the command of General Eisenhower, Allied forces had landed in Morocco and

Algeria. They advanced into Tunisia, but a quick German reaction blocked the route to Tunis.

By March 1943, the Eighth Army had taken Tripoli and crossed into Tunisia. Eisenhower meanwhile had consolidated his forces and developed his lines of communication. By 20 March, the advancing Eighth Army had linked up with Eisenhower.

The enemy perimeter around Tunis was attacked and on 7 May the Allies entered the city. Five days later two hundred and fifty thousand German and Italian troops surrendered.

The battle for North Africa was won.

The end of the desert campaign inevitably led to change for the Long Range Desert Group. The plan was to move the Group to Lebanon where personnel were to be re-trained in mountain warfare, whilst being used also for specialist missions in the campaigns ahead. There were some temporary re-assignments in cases where units had an immediate need for specialist skills.

The Third Battalion of the Welsh Guards had been formed in 1941. It had fought in the North African Campaign and was now being prepared to move on to the impending campaign in Europe. They had adopted the use of the Welsh language for secure communications.

Bryn was a perfect fit.

TWENTY FOUR

Italy – July 1943

The loss of North Africa left Mussolini fearing that Allied forces would cross the Mediterranean and attack Italy. At the end of April the body of a Royal Marine officer had been found off the Spanish Atlantic coast carrying papers which pointed to plans for Allied attacks on Sardinia and in Greece. That information was passed by the Spanish authorities to Nazi intelligence and it was thus to those destinations that re-enforcements were sent, rather than to Sicily, where the Allies in fact landed on 10 July 1943. Within weeks the island was taken. The Atlantic discovery had been engineered by British Intelligence – in Operation Mincemeat – to mislead the enemy. In years to come it would be discovered that the body was in fact that of Glyndwr Michael from Aberbargoed in Wales, who at the time of his death from the effects of the ingestion of rat poison, had been living on the streets of London.

Although northern Italian cities had been experiencing

bombardment, Rome was bombed by Allied forces for the first time. In July, Allied aircraft dropped leaflets over Rome and other Italian cities. They contained a joint message from Roosevelt and Churchill, which was also repeated over the airwaves:

'At this moment the combined armed forces of the United States and Great Britain, under the command of General Eisenhower and his Deputy General Alexander, are carrying the war deep into the territory of your country. This is the direct consequence of the shameful leadership to which you have been subjected by Mussolini and his Fascist regime. Mussolini carried you into this war as the satellite of a brutal destroyer of peoples and liberties. Mussolini plunged you into a war which he thought Hitler had already won. In spite of Italy's great vulnerability to attack by air and sea, your Fascist leaders sent your sons, your ships, your air forces, to distant battlefields to aid Germany in her attempt to conquer England, Russia, and the world. This association with the designs of Nazi-controlled Germany was unworthy of Italy's ancient traditions of freedom and culture – traditions to which the peoples of America and Great Britain owe so much. Your soldiers have fought, not in the interests of Italy, but for Nazi Germany...

Today Germany's hopes for world conquest have been blasted on all fronts... The forces now opposed to you are pledged to destroy the power of Nazi Germany, which has ruthlessly been used to inflict slavery, destruction, and death on all those who refuse to recognise the Germans as the master race.

The sole hope for Italy's survival lies in honourable capitulation to the over-whelming power of the military forces of the United Nations. If you continue to tolerate the Fascist regime, which serves the evil power of the Nazis, you must suffer the consequences of your own choice. We take no satisfaction in invading Italian soil and bringing the tragic devastation of war home to the Italian people; but we are determined to destroy the false leaders and their doctrines which have brought Italy to her present position. Every moment that you resist the combined forces of the United Nations – every drop of blood that you sacrifice – can serve only one purpose: to give the Fascist and Nazi leaders a little more time to escape from the inevitable consequences of their own crimes. All your interests and all your traditions have been betrayed by Germany and your own false and corrupt leaders; it is only by disavowing both that a reconstituted Italy can hope to occupy a respected place in the family of European nations.

The time has now come for you, the Italian people, to consult your own self-respect and your own interests and your own desire for a restoration of national dignity, security, and peace. The time has come for you to decide whether Italians shall die for Mussolini and Hitler – or live for Italy, and for civilisation.'

Some members of his government turned against Mussolini and when the Grand Council met on 24 July, by a majority, a resolution was passed in terms that the King should be asked to resume his full constitutional powers. On 25 July Mussolini was summoned by the King who dismissed him from office. On leaving, he was arrested on the King's orders, being told by the arresting guards that it was for his own safety. The King appointed Marshal Pietro Badoglio, the Duke of Addis Ababa, as the new prime minister.

News of Mussolini's dismissal was largely met with joy amongst the people who hoped this would mean the end of their war. Statues of Mussolini were toppled over. But Nazi troops soon began to flood into the country.

Badoglio had told the Nazis and the people of Italy that the war would continue, but in the background he tried to reach peace terms with the Allies. On 3 September, an Armistice was agreed and it was announced by General Eisenhower on 8 September. The Nazis took immediate steps to take control of Rome and the King and Badoglio fled south to Brindisi, leaving the Italian army without orders. Chaos ensued. Thousands of soldiers deserted and others joined the Resistance.

On the Greek island of Cephalonia, Nazi forces demanded that Italian troops hand over their weapons. They refused and fought against the German troops and the reinforcements who followed. When the Nazis prevailed they executed thousands of Italian soldiers.

Mussolini had been moved around in an attempt to hide his location from the Nazis. He was sent first to the island of Ponza and then to La Maddalena, off the northeastern coast of Sardinia. In August he had been moved to the Hotel Campo Imperatore at a resort in the Gran Sasso mountains in Abruzzo.

On 12 September, using gliders to land at the resort, Nazi paratroopers and the Waffen-SS removed Mussolini from his captors. He was taken to a meeting with Hitler where he agreed to set up a new regime, the *Repubblica Sociale Italiana*. It had its seat in the town of Salò, on Lake Garda and was thus informally known as the *Salò Republic*; it was there that Mussolini found himself eleven days after his rescue.

On 29 September Badoglio signed an '*Instrument of Surrender of Italy*'. Effectively it gave the Allies political, financial and military control over Italy. The detailed terms included the following:

> '*Benito Mussolini, his Chief Fascist associates and all persons suspected of having committed war crimes or analogous offences whose names appear on lists to be communicated by the United Nations will forthwith be apprehended and surrendered into the hands of the United Nations. Any instructions given by the United Nations for this purpose will be complied with.*'

TWENTY FIVE

13 October 1943

At 3pm local time on 13 October 1943 Badoglio made a broadcast to the people of Italy.

'Italians, with the declaration made September 8th, 1943, the Government headed by me, in announcing that the Commander-in-Chief of the Anglo-American Forces in the Mediterranean had accepted the Armistice requested by us, ordered the Italian troops to remain with their arms at rest but prepared to repel any act of violence directed at them from whatever other source it might come. With a synchronized action, which clearly reversed an order previously given by some high authority, German troops compelled some of our units to disarm, while, in most cases, they proceeded to a decisive attack against our troops. But German arrogance and ferocity did not stop here. We had already seen some examples of their behaviour in the abuses of

power, robbery, and violence of all kinds perpetrated in Catania while they were still our allies. Even more savage incidents against our unarmed populations took place in Calabria, in the Puglie and in the area of Salerno. But where the ferocity of the enemy surpassed every limit of the human imagination was at Naples. The heroic population of that city, which for weeks suffered every form of torment, strongly cooperated with the Anglo-American troops in putting the hated Germans to flight. Italians! There will not be peace in Italy as long as a single German remains upon our soil. Shoulder to shoulder we must march forward with our friends of the United States, of Great Britain, of Russia, and of all the other United Nations. Wherever Italian troops may be, in the Balkans, Yugoslavia, Albania, and in Greece, they have witnessed similar acts of aggression and cruelty and they must fight against the Germans to the last man. The Government headed by me will shortly be completed. In order that it may constitute a true expression of democratic government in Italy, the representatives of every political party will be asked to participate. The present arrangement will in no way impair the untrammelled right of the people of Italy to choose their own form of democratic government when peace is restored. Italians! I inform you that His Majesty the King has given me the task of announcing today, the thirteenth day of October, the Declaration of War against Germany.'

By early October 1943 Allied forces had crossed to the Italian mainland from Sicily and had achieved control of the whole of southern Italy. There had been debate between the British and Americans as to the extent to which Italy should become a battle ground. The British favoured a major offensive drawing Nazi forces into the country and weakening their ability to withstand the Allied assault when it came in northwestern Europe.

The British Eighth Army had crossed from the port of Messina, Sicily, to Calabria on the mainland on 3 September 1943. The main landings had been planned for further north at Salerno, from where an assault would be pursued northwest into Naples. Montgomery had not favoured the southerly landing, anticipating it would be a waste of time and resources if, as he believed, there would be no major engagement of them there by Nazi forces. The hope of drawing Nazi forces away from the major landing points further north would then remain unfulfilled. In the end he had been shown to be correct. They had marched three hundred miles to Salerno without major opposition, but were slowed by various challenges along the way including road blocks, mines and demolished bridges.

At Salerno Allied troops had been met with heavy Nazi resistance, but they were able to secure the beach head. The attack on Naples then began on 19 September. Rommel was by then in command of the northern Nazi force in Italy, whilst Kesselring was in charge of the southern forces. Hitler had agreed with Rommel that defending the territory south of Rome was not a priority and, instead, opposition was designed to slow Allied forces whilst defensive lines were put in place. The Allies had entered Naples on 1 October and on 6 October the Fifth Army had reached the Volturno River north of Naples, the river marking the first of the Nazi defensive lines. The Allies would also have to cross the Barbara and Bernhardt lines, before reaching the heavily defended Gustav line approximately one hundred miles south of Rome.

By October 1943 Bryn was based in Sicily. There he was completing training and preparations for an anticipated mission that would require him to parachute into the Italian mainland northeast of Rome, rendezvous with the Resistance, secure information about troop movements and assess enemy strengths in the region.

He first heard news of Italy's declaration of war against Germany as he was returning to barracks after a training parachute drop at the adjoining airfield. He passed an open door to a room from which he overheard an officer briefing a unit. 'The Italian nation has declared war on the Nazis. You need to get it clear in your heads that the Italian soldier is now your friend, not your foe. Do not shoot him.'

As he sat outside his hut that evening watching the sun slowly drop below the horizon, Bryn could not shake from his mind the image of the young Italian soldier he had shot in North Africa when his hiding place had been compromised. That boy had only been one of many Italian soldiers that Bryn had later opened fire upon during the conflict, but the look of disbelief in the young soldier's eyes that had stuck with Bryn ever since, now brought him close to tears.

If things had worked out differently, Bryn reflected, that young boy might have been fighting by his side, rather than against him. True he may have been no more alive now, a Nazi bullet being capable of ending his life with equal certainty, but the thought that political masters could expect confused young men to do their bidding without question, however maniacal the orders, however contradictory they may be from day to day, left Bryn feeling both despair and anger. Whilst those thirsty for power played games, he reflected, the mothers of the pawns so brutally sacrificed wept.

Wales

Italy's declaration of war against Germany was met in many quarters in Britain with a good deal of ridicule. It was not unusual to hear it depicted as Italy trying to save its own skin. 'They're a treacherous lot' or 'they've always been opportunists' were phrases often heard.

There was concern that Badoglio's own past conduct and that of some of those he appointed to office, made them entirely unsuitable now to lead their country. On 14 October, in the House of Lords, Lord Addison asked what undertakings, if any, the British government had entered into with Badoglio and his associates and whether the government had regard to the record of their actions in the past. He added:

'...the reasons for the Italian surrender are not obscure. They are that the Army and the Air Force had been defeated, and that the Navy preferred to shelter in its ports. The Army and the people clearly had no stomach for the fight. In addition, there was, as we might have expected, a growing hatred of the Germans, and, let us hope, some growth of a hope that there might soon be discerned in the distance some delivery from twenty years of oppression. When we have allowed for all these things, however, the outstanding reason of the surrender of the Italians was that they had been defeated. One reminds oneself of these matters not in any vengeful or revengeful spirit, or anything of the kind, but because it behoves us to remember them in the interests of those who have fought with us and who will fight with us still. We must remember, too, that what has happened has been brought about by the heroism and sacrifice of thousands of Greeks, Albanians, Yugoslavs and Abyssinians as well as by the loss of thousands of precious lives – of men from Britain, of New Zealanders, of South Africans, of Australians, of Indians, and of our Allies from the United States. It behoves us not to forget what these people have fought and suffered for.

In a copy of the Ethiopian News, dated October 9, which I have on the Table here, there is this expression of opinion: "We are not impressed very much with the King of Italy, Marshal Badoglio and others discovering in their consciences the justice of the Allied cause when they have been defeated on the field of battle." It is one thing to remember these things and to accept surrender and to behave – as I am sure we shall behave – decently and generously towards the Italian people; but it is quite a different thing to instal people in positions of authority...

At this time it is right, I think, to remember that during the past twenty years neither the King of Italy nor Marshal Badoglio, so far as I know, protested against Mussolini's exploits, and they stood aside whilst unmentionable cruelties were perpetrated on Italian people. Numbers of the best citizens in the land were sentenced to imprisonment and exile; in some cases they underwent torture. I would recall also what happened in Albania and in France, and the administration of gas to the Abyssinians. Against none of these things, so far as I know, was there any protest by those who have so recently been converted to the cause of liberty. A record of this type, however charitable we may be and are, does not inspire us with confidence in these people as leaders along the path which leads to the restoration of personal liberty, to put it no higher than that.'

—

For over three years Ella had been faced with no option but to be patient. To wait. She had become frustrated by her inability to think of action she could take herself to make something happen. Changes to the government's internment policy had brought about practical developments for some already detained only slowly.

When Alberto was released in 1942 he came to see Ella. Although she had read Emi's letters and the reports in the press, it was Alberto's description of the hardships and the horrors of the odyssey he had shared with Emi, that brought it to life.

Emi's letters over the last twelve months had painted a picture of administrative delay, confused records and tribunals for those detained in Australia being a low priority. She couldn't put her finger on it, but she felt that there was something he was not telling her; that he was protecting her from something. How could Alberto and others be home, but Emi still be detained so far away? His letters sought to re-assure her, but some mornings she felt herself on the verge of travelling to London to find someone in Whitehall outside whose office she could camp and from where she would refuse to leave until she was promised that Emi would be released without further delay.

When Italy surrendered to the Allies in September, Ella struggled to calculate what that would mean for Emi. He was detained because he was born an Italian. Was he now to be treated any more harshly than a defeated population? When Italy declared war on Germany in October, formally, Italians were to be labelled as 'co-belligerents' in the fight against the Nazis; they remained liable to prosecution for war crimes when the war was over. But Ella had little interest in the terminology of conflict. She quickly reached the entirely logical conclusion that now, in the day to day fight, as an unambiguous Italian ally of Britain at war, he would be free to come home immediately.

Italy

The resistance movement that had operated in Italy whilst Mussolini remained in power had been largely made up of those connected to long established anti-Fascist organisations. They formed the bedrock of the Partisan groups that then expanded when Italy declared war on Germany.

After the declaration of war some Italian troops elected to join, rather than fight against, the Nazis, but thousands joined the Allies. Others surrendered to the Nazis and many were 'interned' by them, denying them prisoner of war status. Others deserted and waited out the end of the war, but some joined Partisan groups whose numbers were also swelled by young men in the north fleeing Mussolini's attempts to conscript them into his new army of the Salò Republic.

The Partisan groups were active in the centre and north of the country, based often in the hills and mountains and supported by peasant populations. They sought to be a significant thorn in the side of the occupying Nazis, tying up troops away from the front line battles with the Allies and undermining their strength. They fought to be liberated from the Nazis, but also engaged in civil war with Italian Fascists. Those groups who had a communist core also saw themselves as fighting an ideological war against the ruling elite. Inevitably, differences between the groups sometimes led to disputes, but largely they worked together.

The Nazi response, aided by local Fascists, was brutal. For every Nazi killed by Partisans, ten Italians, often civilians from the nearest village, were executed.

Leonardo had been fifty four when Mussolini declared war against the Allies in 1940. He had long had links with anti Fascist groups and now did what he could to aid their war time activities. For a while he remained based at his home in Grezzo, but increasingly he was called upon to assist in operations, gathering information which was then passed on to Allied intelligence. His age somehow made him more convincing and less suspicious in his role as a local who had drunk too much wine if he was stopped during any intelligence gathering mission. He was usually sent on his way with impatience.

In the early months of the war, these groups sometimes secured information by breaking into regional offices of the Fascist Party and passing on communications and membership data they found there, as well as planning sabotage against industrial sites essential to the Fascist military campaign. When the Nazis flooded into the country in 1943, their guerrilla activities extended to attacks on Nazi patrols and gathering intelligence on enemy movements.

As he spent less time at his home, Leonardo became nervous about leaving the *biblioteca* unprotected. He feared Fascist destruction of the collection if found. He therefore packed the books in sealed wooden crates and buried them in the woods, intending to recover them at a later date. He then began spending weeks at a time in the hills, often alone for many days.

Leonardo was happy to see Mussolini side lined, but in many ways the battle had not changed. The enemy remained

Fascism whether it came in the form of the Nazis or the Italians who remained loyal to the Nazi cause. He welcomed the fact of Italy's declaration of war against Germany, but derided the pomposity of the chosen words. He had no faith in Badoglio whose actions in Ethiopia and failure to challenge Mussolini or the Nazis until the nation was all but defeated, made him, in Leonardo's eyes, only a less noisy member of the snake family. No, the hope now lay in the Allied drive northwards through the country. He prayed for their victory and the potential for a new beginning in Italy under the leadership of a young breed of enlightened democrats.

Australia

On 14 May 1943, at approximately 4.10am, AHS Centaur, a hospital ship in the service of the Australian military, had been hit by a torpedo from a Japanese submarine off the coast of Queensland. She sank within three minutes of the strike. Of the three hundred and thirty two personnel and civilians on board, two hundred and sixty eight lost their lives.

The Australian people were outraged that a hospital ship had been attacked in breach of the Hague Convention and the press had presented the shocking news as evidence of the '*limitless savagery*' of the Japanese aggressors.

The news reports that Emi had read of the attack brought back chilling memories of the events he had himself experienced three years earlier. It was all the more shocking in the knowledge that the Centaur had carried the clear insignia of the Red Cross.

The day after he read that report, the back pain that Emi had continued to suffer began to worsen. Maybe that was pure co-incidence. Maybe it was not.

A doctor had examined Emi and prescribed some stronger pain killers. They had helped to make the pain bearable – just – but when Stanley came to visit Emi in August, he saw the undeniable pain he was suffering etched across his face. He had come to tell Emi news of Allied progress in Sicily and the dismissal of Mussolini – all grounds for optimism – and less positive news that his continuing attempts to find evidence that supported Emi's version of events from 1923 had so far been fruitless.

At Stanley's insistence, the camp authorities eventually agreed to transport Emi to Melbourne where his back could be x-rayed. It took another six weeks to organise.

⸺

On 15 October Emi was sat in a waiting area at the hospital in Melbourne, an accompanying guard sat next to him. The journey had been uncomfortable and the pain was now thumbing its nose at the impotent medication he continued to take. It was there that he picked up a newspaper and learnt for the first time that Italy had declared war on Germany.

Throughout the x-ray procedure that news raced around his head, as Emi tried to focus through the pain upon its implications. Italy is now Britain's ally. Does that mean he will now be free to return home? Or does the tribunal's conclusion mean that he is still to be considered a threat to the nation's security as a 'sympathiser' of the unchanging Fascist enemy? He needed to speak to Stanley.

When a doctor came to see him, x-ray results in hand, Emi had to force himself to concentrate on the medic's words. 'I have looked carefully at your results and I can see the cause of your pain.' He held an x-ray up to a light and pointed to a feint fragment. 'It would seem that when you injured your back there was a fracture of a vertebra that did not completely heal. There is a fragment of detached bone as you can see here.'

Emi strained his eyes to see it.

'I have to tell you Mr Magnani that you need surgery. The fragment is dangerously near the spinal cord and could damage it, if not removed. The damaged vertebra will not now be able fully to heal,' he continued pointing again to the x-ray. 'We need to fuse these two vertebrae together.'

'No, no, no' was all Emi heard in his head. 'I need to travel back to Britain as soon as I can,' Emi told the doctor. 'Can I have the surgery when I get there?'

'I cannot advise you to travel that distance in your current condition. You need to understand that if you do, the bone fragment could damage the spinal cord and you could become paralysed from the waist down. At sea you would not have the specialist medical care you would need. My advice is that you rest and we schedule surgery here as soon as the hospital's list allows.'

TWENTY SIX

Moscow - 1943

During the second half of October and into November 1943, the Allies held a conference in Moscow. Over the course of twelve meetings the Foreign Ministers of Britain, the United States of America and the Soviet Union discussed a wide range of subjects.

A number of Declarations were drawn up at the conclusion of the conference. One of them concerned Italy:

'The Foreign Secretaries of the United States, the United Kingdom and the Soviet Union have established that their three governments are in complete agreement that Allied policy toward Italy must be based upon the fundamental principle that Fascism and all its evil influence and configuration shall be completely destroyed and that the Italian people shall be given every opportunity to establish governmental and other institutions based on democratic principles.

The Foreign Secretaries of the United States and the United Kingdom declare that the action of their governments from the inception of the invasion of Italian territory, in so far as paramount military requirements have permitted, has been based upon this policy.

In furtherance of this policy in the future the Foreign Secretaries of the three governments are agreed that the following measures are important and should be put into effect:

1. *It is essential that the Italian Government should be made more democratic by inclusion of representatives of those sections of the Italian people who have always opposed Fascism.*

2. *Freedom of speech, of religious worship, of political belief, of press and of public meeting, shall be restored in full measure to the Italian people, who shall be entitled to form anti-Fascist political groups.*

3. *All institutions and organizations created by the Fascist regime shall be suppressed.*

4. *All Fascist or pro-Fascist elements shall be removed from the administration and from institutions and organizations of a public character.*

5. *All political prisoners of the Fascist regime shall be released and accorded full amnesty.*

6. *Democratic organs of local government shall be created.*

7. *Fascist chiefs and army generals known or suspected to be war criminals shall be arrested and handed over to justice.*

In making this declaration the three Foreign Secretaries recognize that so long as active military operations continue in Italy the time at which it is possible to give full effect to the principles stated above will be determined by the Commander-in-Chief on the basis of instructions received through the combined chiefs of staff.

The three governments, parties to this declaration, will, at the request of any one of them, consult on this matter. It is further understood that nothing in this resolution is to operate against the right of the Italian people ultimately to choose their own form of government.'

TWENTY SEVEN

Italy - 1944

Although Mussolini professed to be in control of his new Republic, in reality he was now no more than a puppet of the Nazi regime. Indeed, his movements and communications were restricted by the SS. He told others he would regain all territorial losses. It seems unlikely he actually believed his own words.

Under pressure from Hitler and loyal Fascists who formed the government of the new Republic, Mussolini had supported a number of executions of some of those who had betrayed him by voting him out in July 1943. Those killed had included his own son in law, Galeazzo Ciano.

The south of Italy was now effectively governed by the Allies. Badoglio and his government held little influence and he was despised by Italian anti-Fascists.

In November 1943 Rommel had been moved to northern France to oversee Nazi defences, leaving Kesselring in sole command in Italy. He was under orders to maintain

Rome under Nazi control for as long as possible. The Allies faced determined Nazi defences. As they worked their way along Route 6, the main road from Naples into Rome, they eventually reached the Gustav Line in mid-January at the small town of Cassino.

In late January Bryn was finally informed that his mission behind enemy lines was ready to proceed. At his briefing he was told that he would parachute at night into the wide valley of the Aterno river, near L'Aquila, about seventy five miles northeast of Rome. He was to rendezvous with Italian Partisans – his contact was code named 'Antonio' – and head southeast in and around the valleys between the mountains towards Sulmona. He was to look for any weaknesses in the Nazi defences, in the hope that in the more difficult mountain terrain there might be routes for Allied forces to flank the defensive lines. It would be folly to launch an assault through the natural defences of the terrain in winter weather, as well as Nazi opposition, in the absence of reliable intelligence.

The drop went smoothly and after burying his parachute behind a thick tree line, Bryn headed for the rendezvous point just outside the village of Pianola. He waited in a derelict barn until he heard the anticipated signal and was soon shaking the hand of his contact. Antonio, who spoke good English, explained that they must move immediately before daylight could interrupt their progress. He led Bryn northeast to a position about half a mile from the river, where they took cover in a small farm building. Antonio left Bryn for a short time whilst he secured food and water from the farmer who was known to be a supporter of the Partisans.

They sat out daylight under cover. To the north Bryn could see the mountains and the high peak of the Corno Grande. To the southwest stretched the forested hills topped by Rocca di Mezzo. In between lay the path of the valley in the direction of the southeast back towards the Nazi defensive lines.

Antonio explained that before he had taken up the fight against Fascism, he had been a student of history in Genoa. In their conversations over the coming weeks, he would demonstrate an understanding of British history that left Bryn feeling embarrassed by his own sometimes superficial knowledge of his country's past.

When he learnt that Bryn was Welsh, Antonio, rather than asking whether he did, simply asserted 'You must play rugby.' It turned out that Antonio had himself played the game in Genoa. He delighted in explaining his love of the game, but spoke too of the Fascist attempts to take ownership of the sport as a promotion of Italian masculinity and the greater value of the group over the individual. Mussolini had even tried to rename the game. He called it *'palla ovale'* – 'oval ball' – asserting that it had its origins in the Roman game of *'harpastum'*.

They both laughed when Antonio explained that Mussolini soon dropped his interest in the game on discovering that those who played it were stubbornly resistant to authority.

Over the next few days, they zig zagged across the valley and up into the hills and mountains on either side, as far as the severe winter conditions would allow them, exploring the terrain and signs of Nazi defences. It quickly became clear that the valley itself could form a trap to any forces moving along it if fired upon from high ground on either side. It was also clear that the road through the valley was in regular use by enemy troops as they moved resources southeast to the Gustav Line.

The troop movements were relayed back to Bryn's point of contact in Sicily. He used the radio he had brought with him and he communicated in Welsh to confuse any Nazi eavesdroppers. The road was ruled out as a safe way in for the Allies and instead Bryn's superiors planned to bomb the road network to disrupt Nazi supply lines. They also planned a bombing raid on a chemical factory at the foot of the mountains near Popoli further southeast along the valley. Bryn and Antonio were ordered to head to the area just outside Popoli and they fed back damage reports after the bombing runs were completed.

They continued their reconnaissance into the mountains east of Popoli, but by the middle of March they had doubled back intending to explore further south. On 22 March they waited under cover in the outskirts of Popoli, in a disused building where they could use the roof to observe the town centre without being detected. Antonio intended to enter the centre of town after dark to secure supplies from a Partisan supporter.

From the roof top, through binoculars, Bryn saw a line of people grow outside the town hall as noon approached.

Antonio explained that they were there to collect rations. Those who lined up appeared largely to be women and children.

The sound of aircraft came suddenly. It may have been because the valley was insulated from the engine noise until the planes were close. Bryn was able to identify the outline of British bombers only an instant before the first bombs struck the town. Antonio pulled Bryn away from the roof top and beckoned him into the building from where they both listened in horror as the heavy bombardment continued.

When it was past, Bryn returned to the roof from where he could see in the distance that the town hall and surrounding buildings had been struck. He could just make out through the dust of demolition twisted figures, both large and small, motionless on the ground where the ration line had been. He wanted to run and help, but Antonio insisted he must stay; Antonio would go. Bryn's presence would simply put him and others at risk if he was seen by the enemy. He did not say it, but Bryn knew that Antonio was uncertain of the reaction a British soldier would receive from even those who supported the Allies in the aftermath of the attack.

Antonio left him. Bryn, unable to help, could not bear to watch. Why the hell did the British bomb the town? He was there gathering intelligence; why didn't they bother to ask him?

Antonio returned close to midnight. The look of devastation on his face told Bryn all he needed to know.

The small town of Cassino sat at the foot of a hill, atop which stood the sixth century Benedictine Monastery of Monte Cassino. Access to the monastery was via a narrow road which zig zagged its way up the hill. The plain below suffered floods from the Liri and Rapido rivers in winter and to the south the Aurunci Mountains completed the barriers that formed the bottle neck along the route to Rome. It was an ideal location for the Nazis to defend.

From the middle of January 1944 Monte Cassino had become the setting for months of brutal conflict. The winter of that year proved also to be one of the worst on record. Over four bloody battles, troops from seven Allied nations struggled to gain the upper hand, until on 17 May the Nazi defences at Monte Cassino finally fell.

By the end of April there was little more Bryn could achieve in his mission. With the improvement in the weather, he was ordered to return south of the enemy line. Antonio guided him through the mountains where he knew he could smuggle Bryn across, particularly as so much of the Nazi defence was now focused on Route 6. Once across the line, Bryn was under orders to cross to the west and join up with the Third Battalion of the Welsh Guards who were engaged in the drive towards Rome.

Bitter news had reached them via Partisan contacts that Nazi reprisals had continued with ever greater brutality.

Following a Partisan attack on enemy troops in Rome on 23 March, there were reports that well over three hundred people had been executed by the Nazis in the tunnels of the disused quarries at Fosse Ardeatine.

Bryn tried to persuade Antonio to join him in crossing to the south, but having spent the last three months with his brave Italian companion, Bryn knew his answer even before the question was asked. His place was with his people where he would continue to make life as difficult as possible for the Nazis during, what he believed would be, their final days in his country.

By the time Bryn reached Route 6, Monte Cassino had fallen and he caught a lift up the line, which was still under attack, to meet up with the battalion. He found them about ten miles beyond Cassino.

After reporting to the commanding officer, he found himself in the passenger seat of an armoured truck, being driven by a private who introduced himself as 'Llywelyn' and then, after a pause, 'The Prince of Wales.' 'Now, I know you'll be asking yourself why I'm known by such an elevated title, so let me clear that up for you before we go any further so that it doesn't bother you for hours to come.'

Bryn was about to reassure His Royal Highness that he wasn't bothered by it in the slightest, but he could see that his companion was in the middle of a well rehearsed monologue that Bryn decided he was too tired to interrupt.

Eventually, after various digressions, Llywelyn described a family tree whose roots had long persuaded him that he was descended directly from a noble line of Celtic warriors, which included links to Llywelyn ap Gruffudd one of the last native Princes of Wales before the title was 'stolen' by the English in 1284. He explained that his sergeant had christened him 'The Prince of Wales' soon after meeting him and had described him, with a degree of sarcasm that was not immediately apparent to Llywelyn, as 'The Welshist Welshman' he had ever met. When Llywelyn turned to his passenger for an acknowledgment of his lauded status, he found him asleep, face pressed against the window.

When they camped that night, Bryn sat quietly writing to Meghan. He could not tell her about the missions he had been on, because he was not allowed to do so. Nor could he tell her about the brutality of war or the brave and fragile lives that had crossed his path, because he could not yet allow himself to do so. He would find the words and share them with her when all this was over.

As he tried to discover new words that would reassure Meghan, Llywelyn sat down beside him and began Chapter Two of 'All Things Welsh'. 'You know, I prefer to write to my sweetheart in Welsh. It's the language of fire and passion, you know.'

Llywelyn took the slightest of tangents and before long was telling Bryn about what happened a few weeks ago. 'We were bogged down under heavy enemy mortars and we radioed HQ with coordinates for fire upon their positions. We communicated in Welsh as always when sending that kind of information. Well, next morning, would you believe it, the Nazis dropped all these leaflets. We couldn't read a word of them, but one of the officers told us they were written in Urdu. Seems Herr Hitler had been listening in, but clearly he has no ear for a language that's not his own. There's a surprise!'

Towards the end of May the battalion was about seventeen miles beyond Cassino. They were once again facing high defended ground on either side of the route; Monte Grande and Monte Piccolo on one side and Monte Oria on the other. Along with the Third Battalion Grenadier Guards and Second Battalion Coldstream Guards, they engaged in heavy fighting, the attack beginning at night and lasting for three days.

The German defenders of the Parachute Division fought fiercely and there were major casualties on both sides. When the Guards finally prevailed, it was with heavy losses.

The blood of the brave that stained Monte Piccolo included that of a most noble Celtic warrior.

Over 4 to 5 June Allied forces liberated Rome from the Nazis.

The King, Victor Emmanuel, named his son, Umberto, as 'lieutenant general of the realm', passing him all powers, albeit retaining the title of King for himself. Badoglio was replaced. The leading anti-Fascist parties formed a nominal government led by socialist Ivanoe Bonomi.

On 6 June, the Allied landings in Normandy began.

TWENTY EIGHT

Kesselring's forces retreated only gradually to the line of the River Arno, almost two hundred miles north of Rome. His objective was to give his forces time to consolidate a further deep line of defence which ran from south of La Spezia on the west coast, through the natural spine defence of the Apennines and across to the Foglia Valley near Pesaro on the east coast.

Those defences had been known as the Gothic Line, but in June 1944 they were re-named the Green Line in response to Hitler's concern that, in view of its historical Germanic links, in the event of an Allied breach the original name would be used to herald claims of a decisive victory.

In addition to the natural defences of the mountains, the line was also being fortified with concrete reinforced gun emplacements, barbed wire and miles of ditches. The Partisans were doing their best to disrupt the preparations. Those who were prisoners and forced to work on the construction, excelled at sabotage and local Italian factories deliberately provided concrete of poor quality. In the mountains the Partisans were effective in attacking Nazi troops and transport behind the construction of the defensive line.

The Nazis were prepared to counter the Partisan resistance through extreme brutality. On 17 June 1944, Kesselring issued an order which effectively granted impunity to commanders who might choose to resort to excesses in operations against the Partisans.

> '... *The fight against the bandits must be carried on with all the means at our disposal and with the utmost severity. I will protect any commander who exceeds our usual restraint regarding the choice and severity of the methods he adopts against partisans. In this connection the old principle holds good: that a mistake in the choice of methods when executing one's orders is better than failure or neglect to act. Only the most prompt and severe handling will be sufficient deterrence to nip in the bud other outrages on a greater scale...*'

In July Bryn was called to force HQ. Commanders had found the intelligence he had secured in his last mission useful and they wanted to repeat the exercise behind the newly drawn enemy lines. He was briefed by a Captain who had been in contact with the Partisans.

'The plan is to drop you at night into the Ceno Valley – here,' the Captain explained as he pointed to the wall mounted map. 'We need to drop you a little further north than is ideal to avoid you falling into the laps of the enemy. There have been clashes between the Partisans and the Nazis in the area, but our intelligence is that the drop zone is currently safe.'

Bryn looked at the map and instantly recognised the valley and the hills that Emi had so often described to him.

'Under darkness you'll be able to make it up to the town of Bardi,' the Captain resumed, 'where you'll find a side door to the church in the main square which will be left open for you. There's a corner room, the door to which you will be able to lock from the inside. Stay there until your Partisan contact comes to you. That should be some time after daylight, but whatever you do, just wait. Don't break cover before he gets to you.'

Bryn felt an odd mix of emotions and struggled to remain focussed on what he was being told. In any other circumstances it would have been a joy to see Emi's birth place, but now he was to arrive in the midst of war. How strange it was that his journey through Africa and Europe should now bring him to Bardi. He forced himself to concentrate on the Captain's words.

'Weather permitting, the mission date is the night of the 16th. Your Partisan contact is code named "Luca".'

Bryn parachuted silently into the Ceno valley as planned on the night of 16 July 1944. The moon was cloud covered for much of the time and the darkness helped him make good progress across initially open ground. Soon he was approaching the climb up to Bardi and as a thinning of the cloud briefly seeped dull moonlight, he saw the heavy, brooding outline of the castle that stood at the top.

He stayed off the road, but followed a parallel line up to the town and after taking time to become aware of the sounds, smells and shadows of the route ahead, he headed quickly to the town square. He paused whilst an elderly man in his vest finished a cigarette and returned indoors and then followed the perimeter of the square until he came to the side door to the church. Inside he briefly took in the layout before heading into the corner room and turning the key he found in the lock.

The room had a small window high up the wall, beyond even Bryn's head height, that he could reach only by standing on a cupboard that rested against the wall. The window looked out onto the square. All was quiet and he saw no sign of any movement that might suggest he had been spotted. He sat in the corner of the room with his back to the wall, facing the locked door, his pistol resting in his hand. In the early hours and, away from the noise of battle for the first time in weeks, the silence seduced him into a shallow sleep.

━━━

Bryn woke with a start when he heard voices in the square. It was barely dawn as he climbed onto the cupboard and cautiously looked out. He saw a number of people beginning their day. In the centre of the square, a young woman spoke to another as her two young children chased each other in a game. At the back of the square he could see an old man smoking; his dog cut short his morning exploration of new overnight smells when his master called that it was time to head off.

Suddenly he heard the sound of aircraft, quickly followed by the start of a siren call that had become a familiar herald of death and destruction during the battles for North Africa. He could hear more than one Jericho trumpet as Stuka dive bombers tuned their instruments and began to fall upon the town.

He knew instantly what was coming. He unlocked and wrenched open the door. He raced into the square waving his arms and calling 'Run for cover' as loudly as he could. Some instinctively did as he demanded, whether they understood him or not, but others looked stunned and confused by the crescendo from above and the giant running towards them shouting in English.

The mother at the centre of the square struggled to pull her two children into her arms. As he arrived Bryn reached for them both and told the mother to run. He followed her closely with a child under each arm as the first bombs began to fall. They ran towards the church, but with each step it seemed that the chasing explosions were getting ever closer. As he approached the door of the church, he felt a shearing hot pain through his leg and his limbs suddenly lost the ability to maintain a forward motion. He fell forward and the last thing he saw was the children spill from his arms into the entrance to the church.

Lieutenant Cartwright could barely find the energy to draw smoke from his cigarette into his lungs as he sat on the ground outside the field hospital south of Pisa where he had struggled for most of the day to save the lives of two broken figures who had so recently been young, healthy Allied soldiers. In the end, he had failed. He was exhausted.

He did not look up at first when he heard the sound of yet another vehicle braking hard and coming to a halt, but the forceful demand for help that came in Italian could not be ignored. Cartwright rose and moved to the vehicle where he found a soldier slumped in the passenger seat, clearly unconscious. The footwell was pooled with blood which had run from the soldiers torn legs even though there was a tight tourniquet in the form of a belt around the left thigh.

The soldier was too heavy for Cartwright to lift alone and the driver of the vehicle immediately stepped to his aid. They carried him in and Cartwright got to work on what looked like another lost cause. His exhaustion prevented him from taking in much beyond his patient, but he noticed the Italian driver step back as if to take a moment to observe that all the help that he could have hoped for was now available to the patient. The grey bearded driver looked in Cartwright's direction and nodded. As the light shifted across his face, Cartwright noticed a crescent shaped scar below his left eye. He nodded back at the Italian who turned and left.

———

When Bryn woke he could smell that he was in a hospital even before his eyes could focus upon the ceiling above him. He felt pain everywhere as his brain tried to locate the source of maximum trauma. When his eyes adjusted, he could look down and focus on the foot of the bed. He blinked a couple of times to clear his vision, but nothing could change the fact that whilst his right foot clearly rose before the bed frame, on the left the view to the frame was uninterrupted.

As he tried to adjust to the loss of his left leg, Bryn told himself in a silent mantra that he was lucky to be alive. He asked the doctor, who sat at his side when he was ready, to fill in the gaps in his knowledge. He was now in a hospital in Perugia. He had been transferred there after surgery at a field hospital outside Pisa and had been unconscious for two weeks. The trauma to his left leg had been so severe that amputation below the knee was the only option. He had lost a lot of blood and had barely survived. If it had not been for the tourniquet and quick reactions of the driver who brought him to the field hospital, he would certainly have died.

The doctor tried his best to answer Bryn's questions, but he had not himself met, nor did he know the identity of, the man who had driven him one hundred and twenty miles and through enemy lines to safety.

TWENTY NINE

Australia – 1944

Emi's surgery was scheduled for January. He was relieved that a date had been fixed and, although no one could honestly say they looked forward to going under the knife, he just wanted it over and done with.

He had found a strange sense of relief in being able to write to Ella with news of his health, as it provided a clear and uncomplicated reason for further delay in any prospect of his returning home soon. He knew he would have to explain everything to her before long, but he hung on to the hope that information would soon be forthcoming to support the truth.

Emi had reassured Ella about his medical treatment in the measured, but positive, language used by his surgeon, who turned out to be a Navy medic. 'There are, of course, risks associated with surgery so close to the spinal cord, but I'm confident it should be mainly plain sailing and, with a fair wind, the pain you have been suffering will be largely put behind you and left on the distant horizon.'

Emi had been warned that there would likely be some loss of flexibility and movement, but not to the extent that it would impact significantly upon his functioning. He might need the support of a stick. It was this that played on his mind in the days before the procedure. He was still in his thirties and did not welcome the thought of any loss of physical ability, but it seemed he had little choice. A repeating nightmare, set on board a sinking ship, came back to haunt him. In this version he could not escape the groaning steel structure as it plunged beneath the waves, his body unable to respond to the urgent demands he tried to transmit through his limbs.

Emi returned to Melbourne and the surgery proceeded as scheduled. Afterwards his surgeon told him that 'The voyage proceeded as planned and we returned to *terra firma* without incident.' A few days later, whilst holding the results of a further x-ray to the light, his surgeon confirmed 'Mission accomplished.'

Stanley came to visit Emi whilst he was still in hospital, armed with fruit and newspapers. They were happy to see each other. For a while it was as if the sterilised atmosphere of the hospital protected them from the war in the outside world and they spoke of things that friends might chat about in a time of peace.

Eventually, though, it came to the subject of Stanley's enquiries. The good news was that as Allied forces progressed through southern Italy, access to all sorts of records was becoming possible. There had, indeed, been examples of unsigned documents being discovered related to Fascist memberships, especially amongst the youth sections, but he had no news that had a direct bearing on Emi's case.

Emi reflected on the reality of his situation. How could he expect Allied forces in Italy, fighting for their lives against the Nazis, to spend any time looking for a needle in a haystack? It was completely unrealistic. It was unfair for him even to contemplate his case being any kind of priority in those circumstances. Stanley, of course, knew that as well; but he was not ready to give up.

———

After several weeks in hospital, Emi returned to camp where he worked daily on the exercises he had been instructed in whilst still under medical care. There were days when he struggled, but on the whole he maintained his mobility with the aid of a walking stick. There were even days when he wondered whether the addition of a walking stick would give him an air of distinction when he finally was able to walk through Tumble's streets once again. He made good progress, but found himself telling Ella in his letters to her that his recovery would take time.

One day in mid June Emi was sat outside his hut, reading an Australian newspaper that was a couple of weeks old. He had found it in a waste paper basket as he passed through the administration building following a brief appointment with the camp doctor to check on his progress. He felt a surge of optimism as he read about the liberation of Rome and the Allied assault on Normandy.

A week before, in a letter from Ella, Emi had received the news that Bryn was fighting in Italy. He felt frustrated that it was his friend, rather than Emi himself, who was risking his life to liberate the country of his birth. But he also felt an overwhelming sense of gratitude. He had always thought of his giant friend as indestructible, but now, five years into a brutal war, he knew that even the luck of the strongest could run out.

'Still got your head in the papers I see,' Stanley said as he walked towards Emi.

'They, you and letters from home are my only windows onto the world out there. It's good to see you. How are you?'

Stanley wore a smile that seemed ready to explode into laughter. Emi looked at him quizzically.

'I have news,' Stanley began. He paused as if composing words he barely believed himself. 'You're a free man.'

Emi looked at his friend, unsure whether he had heard him correctly. He was about to ask him to repeat what he had said when Stanley started laughing. 'You're free. You can go home.'

'How? What do you mean? Have they found some evidence?' spluttered Emi.

'Not that I know of,' said Stanley, shaking his head. 'They just told me you can go. No need for a tribunal or anything like that. Just…off you go!'

They sat together silently taking it in. They speculated that examples of documents now being discovered had led the authorities to accept Emi's version of events, but in the end Stanley suspected 'They just can't be bothered any more. The campaigns in Europe are the focus and they've bigger fish to fry.'

Emi suddenly felt quite deflated. Is that it? He had imagined another day in front of a tribunal, making sure he could say all the things he had failed to say before. But now he was just to go quietly, with nothing more to be said?

Before they parted Stanley said, 'I wrote them a letter. I told them about the man I had come to know. A man whose word could be trusted absolutely. A man who hates Fascism and could never be a threat to a country whose welcome he valued so much when he arrived as a young man. I have no idea whether it made any difference. But they needed to know about my friend.'

When Emi was able to compose himself, he simply said 'Thank you.'

Later that night Emi wrote to Ella. It was a short letter. *I'm coming home!* He wondered whether he, or the letter, would arrive in Tumble first.

———

It wasn't until mid August that Emi was given passage on a merchant ship from Melbourne. Stanley was there to meet him and to wish him farewell. Emi struggled to find adequate words of gratitude for Stanley's belief in him. He did his best.

'I hope we'll find some evidence that puts the record straight one day,' Stanley said.

With the aid of his stick Emi made his way slowly up the gangplank a little nervous about putting his fate once again in the hands of the dangers that waited at sea. But as he waved one last time to Stanley, he imagined that at the top of his climb he would be able, at last, to look down the hill into Tumble.

THIRTY

Paddington – October 1944

When Emi arrived at Paddington Station on a damp October evening, he felt tired but filled with a quiet calm in the knowledge that he was about to embark on the final leg of his journey. He called Ella and cried silently as he sank into the enveloping warmth of her familiar voice. The children shouted excitedly in the background and Ella knelt, holding the phone so that Emi could hear a new voice say, 'Hello daddy.'

Emi had laughed aloud when he discovered that he had a long wait on a cold bench for the morning train to the west. He sank stiffly and slowly onto his seat with the steadying aid of his walking stick. He didn't care that his bones ached. Even the coffee tasted good. He took in the sights, sounds and smells of the station.

Even though the country was still at war, Emi felt safe. So safe, that he soon drifted into sleep.

The pain that shot down his back caused Emi to cry out as he felt himself being lifted by his collar from behind. The pain quickly turned to anger and then to disbelief as he turned unsteadily with the aid of his stick to look at the cause of his discomfort.

The two men looked at each other silently for a few moments. It was as if in the face of the other they saw for the first time the toll they had themselves paid for the adversities of the last five years. As Emi took in the crutches under the arms and the shortened limb that hung alongside, he knew that the shape before him remained unmistakeably Bryn.

They embraced without words, reluctant to let go. When they did they laughed and wiped tears from their eyes.

Without needing to explain, neither chose to speak about their wars as they travelled home. There would be time enough for that. Instead they talked about the things they had missed and the things they longed now to do. And when they ran out of things to say, they slept peacefully.

THIRTY ONE

Italy – 1945

Florence had fallen to Allied forces in August 1944. The Green Line lay in wait and then beyond, not until April 1945 did the Allies finally cross the River Po, the final line of Nazi defence in the north. By the time of the Nazi surrender on 8 May 1945, ending the war in Europe, the Guards had reached the Italian-Austrian border.

Mussolini had largely disappeared from view. He had made his last speech in Milan in December 1944. By April 1945, with Allied forces now quickly advancing through the north of the country, he and his mistress, Clara Petacci, tried to escape across the Swiss border. Mussolini wore a disguise, but having spent years ensuring his own distinctive image was published, painted and photographed across the nation and beyond, they were easily identified and captured by Italian Communist Partisans.

Although the terms of the September 1943 surrender required Mussolini to be handed over to the United Nations, he and Petacci were executed by firing squad on 28 April near Lake Como. Their bodies were taken to Milan where they were strung upside down at a service station along with the bodies of a number of other leading Fascists.

THIRTY TWO

Wales - 1946

In the early spring of 1946, two men could be seen pitch side raising their wooden supports in the air as they swayed unsteadily and celebrated Tumble's fourth Challenge Cup. At the pub afterwards they shared in a moderate amount of excess.

Almost a year after the war had ended, Bryn and Emi were still savouring each new day with their families. On the days when it felt like their past experiences hung darkly over the present, they would meet and listen quietly, as trauma was unpacked, without judgment or resolution.

The stories of wartime loss of life had remained overwhelming. Emi had read about the sinking of the German military transport ship MV Wilhelm Gustloff in January 1945, when a Soviet submarine had fired upon her in the Baltic Sea. It was estimated that there were over ten thousand Germans on board the overcrowded ship, of whom almost nine thousand were civilians, including evacuees from eastern European countries, fleeing the Russian advance. He could barely believe that the estimated number of dead stood at nine thousand four hundred.

But, of all the news that Emi had read and listened to as the war had approached its final chapter, none had affected him more deeply than the ten minute BBC report he listened to on 19 April 1945. The introduction concluded with the words *'I find it hard to describe adequately the horrible things that I've seen and heard but here unadorned are the facts...'* Richard Dimbleby then described what he had found at Bergen-Belsen.

Emi was unable to sustain any feelings of bitterness for the way in which he and his fellow internees had been treated. How could he not be grateful to a country that had finally stood against the evil of Fascism and to its people, such as Bryn, who had given so much in the fight?

But his forgiveness was not unconditional. Only if the lessons of the past were learnt and never forgotten, could he truly forgive.

He often thought of those who had touched his life in the years of war. Those now dead had been denied the opportunity to contemplate forgiveness. None of those alive remained unscarred by their experiences.

Cesare Bianchi had been released from internment on the Isle of Man in December 1942. He was re-united with his two children and sister-in-law, Mary, who had been looking after them. Having by then been out of the restaurant trade for a number of years, he was able to find work at Smithfield Market. On 8 March 1945 both he and Mary were among the one hundred and ten people who died when a V2 rocket struck the Market. It was one of the last attacks the Nazis made on Britain.

Stanley stayed in Australia after the war. He married a local language teacher and together they raised four multi-lingual children. He stayed in Government service for a few years and occasionally wrote to Emi telling him that he was still looking out for information that might lead to his records from 1923. When he decided to leave the service and teach instead, he wrote to Emi apologising for the fact that he would no longer have the ability or authority to investigate any further. Emi wrote back telling his friend that he had nothing to apologise for and that he was certain he would be a great teacher.

Alberto and his family remained in Bristol where he and Isabella ran the restaurant for years to come. His *gelato* made them a fortune.

Gus's body was never found. His name remained proudly above the café window. Together with his moustache. Inside the café Emi placed a framed photograph of his uncle on the wall. A plaque with just his name on it was attached to the wall below the picture. Emi did not want his uncle to be remembered just as a man who died on the SS Arandora Star. If a newcomer to the café asked about the impressive man with a friendly smile in the picture, Emi would tell them about Gus's life. Only when that was done would he acknowledge the tragic way in which it was lost.

Emi often wondered whether Bryn's intended contact in Bardi in July 1944 had been Leonardo. He wrote to Leonardo after the war, but thus far he had received no reply. Then in October 1946 Emi received a letter from a lawyer in Parma. The lawyer had enclosed a sealed envelope with Emi's name hand written on the front. He recognised Leonardo's hand. He opened the envelope to find a letter.

'My dear friend

If you are reading this letter it means you have survived the war and the dark shadow of Fascism has been chased beyond Italy's borders. The thought of both brings me hope and joy as I write this.

That this letter has been sent to you also means, I am afraid, that I will not be there with you to see the dawn of a new age of optimism.

By the time you read this letter my lawyer will have acted on my instructions to recover the biblioteca from its hiding place. This letter's arrival also means that he has now arranged for the books to be donated to a local school where I hope they will be loved and well used.

I am hopeful that the new Italy will be driven by values of kindness, equality and the virtue of preserving the treasures to be found in the written word. But it would be remiss of me not to learn, as our nation must, from our inadequacies of the past. So, for that reason, just in case there sadly comes a time when the value of a book is remembered only for the monetary value placed upon it, I have made an arrangement that enables the school to receive the incentive of a small sum each year for so long as the books are preserved in their original form.

A second condition requires the school to allow you and any of your family to visit the biblioteca's new home whenever you wish. I hope you will. I know times will be hard after the war, so if you need it, I have made provision for my lawyer to make some funds available to you when you arrive. Bring your family to see where you were born and where we shared happy days with our noses endlessly between the pages. Tell them your story.

Your friend and fellow custodian,
Leonardo'

The accompanying letter from the lawyer confirmed the devastating news.

'...I do not know how familiar you might be with Leonardo's war time activities. He fought with the Partisans from 1943 and prior to that had worked with anti-Fascist groups in achieving what little they could under the watchful eye of Mussolini's servants. He was involved in many operations through 1943 and 1944.

You will no doubt be aware that as the Nazis retreated in '44 they carried out brutal reprisals against Partisans and civilians alike. At the end of September that year, Leonardo was in the village of Marzabotto which the Nazis proceeded to destroy. It's estimated that around eighteen hundred people were killed. I am sorry to tell you that Leonardo was among them...'

THIRTY THREE

Italy – 1947

In Paris on 10 February 1947, Italy and the Allies signed the '*Treaty of Peace with Italy*'. It came into effect on 15 September 1947.

It was an extensive document dealing with wide ranging issues, but in a few short paragraphs the recitals at the beginning of the document outlined succinctly Italy's contortions through the years of war:

> '*Whereas Italy under the Fascist regime became a party to the Tripartite Pact with Germany and Japan, undertook a war of aggression and thereby provoked a state of war with all the Allied and Associated Powers and with other United Nations, and bears her share of responsibility for the war; and*
>
> *Whereas in consequence of the victories of the Allied forces, and with the assistance of the democratic elements of the Italian people, the Fascist regime in Italy was*

overthrown on July 25, 1943, and Italy, having surrendered unconditionally, signed terms of Armistice on September 3 and 29 of the same year; and

Whereas after the said Armistice Italian armed forces, both of the Government and of the Resistance Movement, took an active part in the war against Germany, and Italy declared war on Germany as from October 13,1943, and thereby became a co-belligerent against Germany; and

Whereas the Allied and Associated Powers and Italy are desirous of concluding a treaty of peace which, in conformity with the principles of justice, will settle questions still outstanding as a result of the events hereinbefore recited and will form the basis of friendly relations between them, thereby enabling the Allied and Associated Powers to support Italy's application to become a member of the United Nations and also to adhere to any convention concluded under the auspices of the United Nations...'

Within the ninety Articles and seventeen Annexes of the Treaty were provisions that included a renunciation of any claim Italy might have over Ethiopia and an obligation to make *'reparations'* to Ethiopia to the value of twenty five million US dollars in the form of goods and services over a period of seven years.

Article seventeen of the Treaty provided as follows:

'Italy, which, in accordance with Article 30 of the Armistice Agreement, has taken measures to dissolve

---

In the autumn of 1947 Emi took his family to Bardi. He had asked Bryn if he wished to come too. In time Bryn would be ready – would need – to travel to Italy again; but not yet.

The children loved the train journey and the stories their father told them. In Bardi they laughed with excitement as they ran through the castle and the hills Emi and Luca used to explore. Bomb damage was still visible in places and the horror of Bryn's tale of his time there sent a chill through Emi as he stood in the square facing the church.

Throughout the journey Emi had thought about finding Aldo Pavani. He was unsure whether he wanted to. When he made tentative enquiries at the post office, a few days after arrival, he was told that Signor Pavani had died during the war.

Emi contacted the head master of the local school. They arranged to visit a few days before they were due to return home. When Emi and his family arrived at the school the headmaster led them across an open space to a door with glass panels which opened into the school library. As they walked he explained to Emi that they had placed the books in a separate room just off the main library, so that the collection could stand in its original form. A hand written catalogue had accompanied the books and they had arranged them according to its contents. All the books were there, save one.

The headmaster left them alone after showing them in. On seeing the shelves, Emi took a deep breath and was surprised when he heard himself saying, 'There you are.'

Emi slowly walked along the shelves running his finger along the spines of old friends, some now more damaged than his own. He pulled out volumes for the children to look at, before replacing them in their allocated spaces. When he reached the end of the shelves, he found the catalogue. He remembered the debate he and Leonardo had about the book on the 1896 battle of Adwa. Back then Leonardo had given in to his fellow custodian, but reminded him he could always change his mind. Emi found the book and slid it off the shelf. He found it a new home in the politics section and, taking a pen from his pocket, he made the necessary amendments in the catalogue.

Emi followed the line of books until he spotted the gap that had been left for the missing volume. He reached in his pocket and pulled out a paper bag. He removed the book inside and looked one final time at the inscription inside the sleeve. He then pushed *'Funghi Nativi Italiani'* into the gap. It was a perfect fit.

As they left the library Adelina pulled at her father's jacket. 'Why have you left your book in there?' It was a book he had shown her many times.

Emi took her hand in his, 'This is where it belongs.'

In memory of all those lost on the SS Arandora Star.

There are some differences in the accounts of the estimated number of lives lost on the SS Arandora Star. Researched sources place the total at 745.

Of that number, 58 were officers and crew (including the Captain), 95 were military guards, 146 were German or Austrian and 446 were Italian.[3]

Among the Italian dead were 65 men, living in the UK, who are known to have been born in towns and villages in the Province of Parma, including the municipality of Bardi:

Bartolomeo Antoniazzi	Giovanni Fulgoni	Giovanni Piscina
Bartolomeo Basini	Vincenzo Gadeselli	Antonio Rabaiotti
Antonio Belli	Andrea Gazzi	Bartolomeo Rabaiotti
Attilio Berni	Francesco Gazzi	Domenico Rabaiotti
Giuseppe Capella	Lino Gazzi	Francesco Rabaiotti
Carlo Capitelli	Luigi Giovanelli	Luigi Rabaiotti
Eduardo Capitelli	Enrico Giraschi	Luigi Raggi
Francesco Carini	Luigi Gonzaga	Lazzaro Ricci
Giuseppe Carini	Giovanni Longinotti	Flavio Rossi
Giovanni Carpanini	Vittorio Lusardi	Giovanni Rossi
Giuseppe Carpanini	Giovanni Marenghi	Luigi Rossi
Giovanni Cavalli	Pietro Mariani	Giovanni Sidoli
Emilio Domenico	Gioacchino Menozzi	Luigi Sidoli
Chiappa	Giacomo Minetti	Luigi Solari
Guido Conti	Luigi Morelli	Antonio Spagna
Giuseppe Conti	Ernesto Moruzzi	Giuseppe Sterlini
Diamente Costa	Peter Moruzzi	Marco Sterlini
Giuseppe Del Grosso	Pietro Moruzzi	Giovanni Strinati
Giulio Felloni	Giuseppe Orsi	Giovanni Tambini
Guido Ferrari	Giuseppe Parmigiani	Ettore Zanelli
Giacomo Franchi	Domenico Pellegrini	Antonio Zanetti
Giacomo Fulgoni	Luigi Pinchiaroli	Luigi Zazzi

May the stories of their lives and the lessons from their deaths, never be forgotten.

---

3 See Appendix to 'Arandora Star. Dall'oblio alla memoria/From Oblivion to Memory' – Maria Serena Balestracci.

If you are interested in reading more about internment in Britain during the Second World War, you may like to read:

Collar the Lot! by Peter and Leni Gillman
Arandora Star. Dall'oblio alla memoria/From Oblivion to Memory by Maria Serena Balestracci

– and see the materials at:

The Warth Mills Project www.warthmillsproject.com

If ever you find yourself in Bardi, please take the time to visit the cemetery where you will discover a small chapel, built to commemorate the victims of the sinking of the SS Arandora Star. It was created and is lovingly maintained by the *Comitato Pro Vittime Arandora Star* and the citizens of Bardi.

My thanks to all those who have patiently helped me in the writing of this book.